KAT DRUMMOND BOOK FIVE

DARKNESS BECKONS

NICHOLAS WOODE-SMITH

ISBN: 9781713314431

Contents

Chapter 1. Evergreen

My name is Candace Evergeen. I have hazel eyes and blonde hair. I like sugared cereal and cats. While I have not finished school, I am regarded as quite smart. At least I hope I am. I do read. A lot. In my 14 years, I have killed sixteen people. My servants have killed around nine hundred and thirty-six. A small part of me says I should regret this.

I do not. At least, I don't think I do.

My story starts in a sleepy suburb of Hope City called Plumstead. About five years ago. On the day that my parents died in front of me.

The afternoon sun was warm on my face as I waited for my dad to fetch me from school. The sky was reddening and the day was growing late. My dad was late. Again. There was no bus to take me. And I had no money for a taxi. The school was too far from my home and I had been told (without any room to argue) that I was, on no condition, to walk home. I didn't understand that. It wasn't as if it was a dangerous neighbourhood. Compared to the rest of Hope City, Plumstead was positively tranquil. There was only the occasional mugging. And never monsters. Well, seldom monsters. I learnt in school that rift-surges could happen anywhere. Anytime. That was why I couldn't go out alone. During the day or the night. I didn't know what difference it made. If a surge could happen anytime, anyplace, then they could just as easily spark in my classroom or in my dad's car. I was in just as much danger anywhere else than I would be if I could walk home.

But my dad insisted that he pick me up from school. He promised he'd be on time. Even when he was late every other day. Even when I joined the chess club and stayed late to help the teachers, he was still late. Not minutes, but hours. Every day. I only came home on time when my mom fetched me. I hated when she couldn't.

The sun waned, lending a melancholic hue to the empty street outside my school. Nobody else was there anymore and the security guard had gone to get more coffee – leaving me alone. I sighed. There was nothing as dreadfully gloomy as an empty school, late in the afternoon. I checked my watch. A cute, pink thing that my mom got me for my birthday the year before. Some of the girls in my class called it childish. Too childish for a nine-year old. I didn't care. I liked it, and that's what mattered. Even though I liked the watch, I felt tears well up as I watched the minute-hand twitch. 6:01pm. My dad had never been this late before, and I could not help but contemplate the worst. The anxieties that permeate any precocious child.

A car finally whizzed around the corner, almost knocking over a trash-can. A red Corsa. It stopped in front of me, and I fought down my anticipated tears, rather bringing up my other feelings – dejection, anger, irritation. I'd been waiting for hours! Longer than ever before.

My dad opened the passenger door from the inside and I threw my bag in and entered without a word. I didn't plan on saying anything, but before I could, my dad smiled. I didn't note it at the time, but I now remember it as looking somewhat sad.

"Hi Candy. How was school?"

"Dad! I told you not to call me that. My name is Candace."

He grinned, mischievously and almost a bit naughtily. "How can I not call you Candy when you're so sweet…"

He reached over to tickle me, and I swatted his hand away. My expression darkened.

"Why are you late? School finished 4 hours ago. Chess finished 3 hours ago. And the last teacher left an hour ago."

My dad reached back to the steering wheel. He maintained the façade of casual joviality, but even then, I saw that something was eating at him.

"I'm sorry, Candy. It's just…lost track of time. Work."

I rolled my eyes. *Work* seldom meant work. It more often meant golf, or drinks with the guys, or all manner of other non-work-related activities. Well, that's what my best friend told me. Her mom left her dad because of drinking. I couldn't say what my dad's job was, and he always avoided answering me when I asked him, so I assumed he didn't work at all. When I needed to bring a parent to showcase their job, I brought my mom. She worked from home, producing scrolls for wizards. It wasn't as impressive as some other kids' parents, but it was better than whatever my dad wasn't doing.

I looked at my dad as he considered the windscreen. Finally, he turned the car back on and we drove home in a deathly silence. My dad turned on the radio, but none of the music playing was any good. I turned it off.

It was dark when we finally fought through traffic and arrived outside our home. We lived in a quiet street. Lights were on in almost every house. Except ours.

"Isn't mom home?" I asked, breaking the silence.

My dad stopped the car on the street, not turning into the driveway.

"She's supposed to be…" he trailed off, and I noted a cold edge to his voice. Ignoring my displeasure with him, I asked.

"Dad, what's wrong?"

"Stay in the car, Candace."

"Dad?"

"Stay in the car!"

My dad grabbed his bag from the backseat and quickly deposited something from the front of the bag into his pants-pocket.

I watched him trot to the front door of the house, over our green lawn, recently watered by a local hydromancer. He opened the door, and entered, not closing it behind him.

I watched, not breathing. My heart beat so fast it felt like it was going to burst out of my chest. I thought myself knowledgeable about the world. But I had no idea what was happening now.

My dad did not return to the car, and I heard nothing from inside the house. The light had come on. From outside, it looked normal.

A thought crossed my mind. What if everything was okay and he'd just forgotten to come fetch me again? I felt the sting of irritation and unbuckled my seatbelt. It would be typical of him to leave me inside the car. And if the light was on, and there was no noise, then nothing could be the matter.

I didn't lock the car. He'd have to come out to lock it. A small atonement. I crossed over the lawn, stopping to hear anything inside. Nothing.

The front door was still open. My lit foyer looked normal. I stood at the threshold and entered. As my ears passed the frame of the door, my senses were shocked by the sudden noise of weeping, crashing, fleshy thuds, and crunching. Faced with this new experience, I didn't know what to do. I should have run. Despite not thinking myself a child, I very much was one. But I also knew that the one weeping was my mother. And I knew I had to do something.

I dropped my bag near the front door and hesitantly walked into my house, towards the noise coming from the dining room. I turned the corner at the end of the passage, to the view of my father entangled with a black clothed man. In my father's hand was a pistol. Something you'd see in a movie, not in your dad's hand. Especially if he wasn't a cop, a monster hunter, or a soldier. To my knowledge, my dad was none of those things. The black clothed man held my dad's wrists, preventing him from aiming the gun. Another black clad man lay slumped up against the far wall, bullet-holes in his chest. I looked around for my mother. She was tied up to a chair, fallen on its side.

I couldn't help but cry out, "Mom!"

My outburst caused my dad and the assailant to turn their heads to me. My dad wasn't distracted for long. He kneed the man in the groin. The man let go of his wrist, and he aimed the gun at the man's head. I saw a split second of hesitation, and then he fired.

There seemed to be a long silence after the man fell to the ground. His head hit the side of the table as he fell, twisting it. As young as I was, I knew that he was dead. Twice over.

The silence was broken by clapping, from right behind me.

"Candace!" my mom cried.

"Get away from her!" my dad yelled, aiming his pistol at someone behind me.

I looked up to see a man with a greying black goatee and wearing a black business suit with a purple tie, looming over me. Before I could move forward, the man grabbed me by the shoulders. My father pulled the trigger of his gun but was rewarded with a click. He reached for his pocket.

I felt the cold bite of metal on my neck. I knew it must've been sore, but I didn't feel anything as mundane as pain. The novelty and terror of the situation prevented any of that.

"I wouldn't do that, Mr Evergreen," the man behind me spoke, calmly. His voice was smooth. Like honey. Yet how could something so smooth and sweet feel so poisonous? My dad stopped with his hand in his pocket. My mom suppressed a sob.

The man moved forward, shoving me further into the room. With every jolt, the bite of the knife became increasingly painful.

"Mr Evergreen," the man continued, with a tone as if he was speaking to a business colleague. "You're a hard man to track down."

"Let go of my daughter," my dad responded, his tone composed, but dripping with rage. His voice didn't sound

12

like honey. It crackled like electricity. The pistol was still pointed at the man in black, despite it being out of bullets.

I stepped over a black clad corpse as the man behind me advanced closer, shoving me.

"Let her go!" my mom cried out.

"All in due time, my dear," the man in black responded. "But first, I insist that Mr Evergreen takes a seat."

My dad didn't move.

"I said…take a seat." My dad cried out in pain as the man in black pointed at him. Just pointed, and uttered a simple, inhuman phrase that sent a genuine shiver down my spine. It sounded nothing like honey.

"Dad?" I asked. I hated the pathetic tone in my voice. I still hated it.

My dad looked at me and tried to speak, before screaming again. He collapsed to his knees, his limbs twisting and twisting. Like a shrivelling insect. I was good at biology. I knew they shouldn't be moving like that. Sweat cascaded down his forehead like a waterfall. He tried to mouth something, but it came out as gasps and cries.

"Stop! Please…" my mom sobbed.

Only I didn't speak, as my dad's body was warped, all over the floor.

Finally, with a click of the man in black's fingers, and another simple phrase, my dad fell to the ground, rasping, but no longer screaming.

"The last member of the League's central command," the man in black said, almost reverently. "I must say, I respected you, Mr Evergreen. You held out for so long. Even after Chairman Dawi was no longer Chairman, and no longer cared about you. Even after the Black Wolf disappeared. As every one of your compatriots fell, you continued to remain elusive."

The man withdrew his blade from my throat and lifted my mother's chair, so she was sitting upright. I didn't think to run. The man could just use his spell on me. I saw the blood-specked spittle around my dad's mouth and knew I didn't want that. And if I ran, and managed to get away, then my parents would die.

"Please…" my mother whispered. "She hasn't done anything to you. Please, let my daughter go. She's innocent."

"Innocence?" the man in black pondered. "Innocence is just a time of plotting. A false passivity before violence. There is no innocent. There are only combatants and bystanders. And bystanders can become combatants. At any time. When they realise that they can. All the world's a battlefield. And we are its soldiers."

He shook his head and continued. "No. You cannot go from combatant to bystander and think that we will leave you alone, Mr Evergreen. As long as one member of the League draws breath, we know that it can begin anew. That its insidious grasp will once again threaten our interests."

My dad looked me in the eyes, from his place on the floor and, for the first time in my life, I felt that I saw him for the first time. He wasn't a deadbeat. He was angry. He was sad. He had done things. But more than that, he was strong. And the look in his eyes told me: "I'll protect you. No matter what it takes."

"The League is dead," my dad said, simply. "I couldn't work against whoever you are even if I wanted to. And I don't care anymore. I just want to live my life. With my family."

"I find that hard to believe. And I find it particularly hard to believe that you don't know who I work for."

"I told you. I don't care. Just…please. Leave my family alone."

"Tsk, tsk, Mr Evergreen." The man in black shook his head. "Lying? In front of your daughter. That is no way to raise a child."

"I'm not lying! I live for my family now. I don't give a shit about Victorum, or the Magocracy, or the Empire, and definitely not the fucking Conclave."

There was a pause, and then the man in black laughed.

"You are growing careless, Mr Evergreen. And while swearing in front of your daughter, you give me the evidence I need."

My dad's face paled. I didn't know what he'd said wrong. He sounded like he was telling the truth. But he'd never sworn before.

"You shouldn't know about the Conclave, Mr Evergreen," the man in black said, simply.

My mother swivelled her head to look at my father, prostrate on the floor.

"You said you quit!" she cried, anger and despair intermingling.

My dad glared at the man. I knew that if he still held his gun, the man would be dead.

"You lie to your family and to me, Mr Evergreen. And where has that gotten you?"

"The Council won't fall to your kind," my dad said, his voice stoic. It was the most confident I'd ever heard him. "Hope City will survive. You won't win!"

The man laughed. "Oh, my dear Mr Evergreen…"

He clutched me by the shoulder and threw me into my dad's arms. The impact winded me but I still managed to look up as he signed words of darkness into the air.

"I don't think you understand."

He loomed over us. Darkness grew all around and became an increasingly growing shadow.

"We've already won."

***

My vision cleared as the darkness receded and the miasma lifted. The first thing I saw sent my mind reeling. I screamed. And kept screaming. I struggled against invisible restraints, as if my limbs had fallen asleep. I didn't stop trying to move. I didn't stop screaming, as I watched my mother's body, pinned to the roof above me, drip blood onto mine.

"Candace! Close your eyes. Close your eyes! Don't look. It's going to be over. It'll stop. Just don't look."

I heard my dad's voice, but it was choked down by screaming. The same screaming from before. And between every scream, I heard the incantation. It's twisted words. They felt like acid on my brain. How could words hurt so much?

I didn't close my eyes. I tried to twist my head. To see my dad. To see the man in black. Blood dripped onto my face. My mother had been screaming. Her eyes were angry, and sad, and despairing. And I'd remembered that I'd forgotten to tell her that I loved her that morning. I'd forgotten to hug her goodbye. I'd been in such a rush. But it didn't matter anymore.

"Dad!" I cried out, as pain wracked me, sending an electric shock through my bones. "Daddy help me!"

"I'll kill you!" I heard him shout. "Leave her alone. I'll kill every single one of you! Every…"

He roared in pain again. I heard a laugh, filled with venom.

"As if I'd give you the chance. Or her. My only decision now is if to kill you first, so she can watch her last parent die, or if I should force you to watch me drain her blood drop by precious drop. The blood of the youth works so well for blood-shaping."

My dad's screaming stopped. His panting was laboured. Painful.

"I know…" the man continued. "The latter option. I hear it is the worst thing for a parent to watch their child die. A worthy atonement for opposing us."

"No! Kill me. Let her go. She can't do anything to you. She won't. She's just a child."

"And children grow old, Mr Evergreen. And when they grow old, they begin thinking about all manner of foolish things…"

The man came into my view. I could see the blood all over his face and hands. If the lights hadn't gone out, I'm sure I'd have seen darker stains on his already dark suit.

"If an injury has to be done to a man it should be so severe that his vengeance need not be feared, Mr Evergreen. And what is so injurious as the killing of parents and children? No. I cannot allow more seeds to take root. You will all die here."

I didn't think about what the man was saying about me. I didn't understand death. But I understood the roar that my father released as he burst from his bonds, despite the pain, and despite the lacerations all over his flesh, and tackled the man to the ground. I felt feeling return to my limbs, and I looked up.

My dad continued to roar, beating the man with his fists, leaving the man's nose bloody. I crawled off the table, backing away as my father primally beat the man. I felt fear, disgust, but also pride. And above all that: shame. Shame that I'd never trusted my dad before. I didn't know what he was willing to do, and had done, to protect me.

My father flew back as suddenly as he had tackled the man in black. I cried out, and the man turned to me. My father rose, but then fell, as the man muttered a word that seared my brain.

I felt a stab in my chest. Worse than any physical pain. I saw the light in my father's eyes go out. His chest heaved one final time. And then stopped.

"A shame," the man in black said, inbetween gasps. "I really wanted him to watch you die."

He lunged at me, from across the room. My mother dripped blood onto the table. My father lay dead. The room was dark.

I don't know why I said it, or even how, but I screamed the words that had been used to torture my father. The man in black's eyes widened, and he fell to the ground, clutching his belly even as his neck twisted and legs convulsed. I screamed the words again, even as they felt like ingested acid and brimstone. They hurt my head, like nothing else ever had before. I felt the darkness grow in the room. More. And more. Until there was no light. And I no longer needed light. The man's scream surpassed my father's. And I didn't stop repeating the words, even as my voice grew hoarse, and the man stopped screaming, and his body stopped reeling. I didn't stop, even as the words no longer felt like fire in my mind.

The darkness abated as I could no longer speak. I could hear noise from outside. Distant traffic. Dogs barking. Too loud neighbours arguing about a TV show. Why had they not come to help? Why hadn't they heard us?

Why were my parent's dead?

I stumbled forward. Step by step. I lurched, and collapsed by my father's side, onto my knees.

"Dad?" I asked, even though I knew he was dead. The cuts all over his body, like some macabre artwork, no longer bled. It was as if his heart had just stopped.

But it couldn't have.

They couldn't be dead. Parents weren't meant to die. Death was for book characters. Death was for your goldfish. Moms and dads weren't meant to die. They weren't meant to leave their daughter alone.

I tried to cry, but I couldn't. And I hated myself that I couldn't.

"I'm sorry," I choked out. "I'm sorry. I'm sorry…"

I repeated myself. Over and over. No tears came, no matter how much I wanted to cry.

I didn't look up as I heard footsteps behind me and felt a reassuring hand on my back.

"What happened, miss?" the voice asked. The voice was elegant. Sounded British. Posh. Like from some old BBC show.

The hand let go, and I looked up. Even in the dark, I could see his features. Pale skin. Black, spiky hair. Younger than my parents. He wore a black suit, like the man. I dived away and tried to remember the words I'd used to stop the man in black. The words didn't come to me.

"Calm down…" the man said, and I couldn't help but find his voice soothing. "I'm not one of them. I'm a friend…of your father's."

He indicated the man in black, twisted like a broken insect on the floor. Had I done that to him?

"Did you do this?"

I hesitated, and then nodded. Slowly.

He contemplated the corpse, and then my parents on the floor and roof.

"He…he did this…" I managed to choke out. "He took them from me."

"I see," he said, simply, and walked towards me.

I didn't back away or break his stare.

"Do you want to bring them back?" he asked.

I didn't understand what he was saying, but a part of me nodded.

"No matter the cost?"

The cost? I had lost everything. I looked into my father's dead eyes. I would give anything. Anything I had left. And everything else.

"Yes," I replied. "I'll do anything."

The man smiled, faintly. "Then we have work to do."

Chapter 2. Darkness

Evil never just happens. There's always a reason. Always something lost. Always a story behind every atrocity. Always a chain. A domino effect of tragedy. I came to understand this about evil. To learn that the world has black, and white, but also a lot of grey.

In the confines of a windowless cell, lit by a single light-bulb on a bedside table, I didn't ponder good or evil. I didn't ponder the blend or the niceties. I only recalled the sight of the one I loved, as his head was torn from his shoulders. And while I felt sadness, I also felt rage. I had said I'd kill the man responsible. And I would. No matter the cost.

"Kat?" I heard a faint voice whisper, from the back of my mind. I sat on the floor, back pressed up against a bed with fresh linen. It smelled of lavender. Opposite me was a small bookshelf, with a random assortment of books from young adult and teen romances to mechanic magazines. It was as if someone had built the petite library from garbage diving. A single flower was placed in a thin vase on top of the shelf. A tulip.

"Kat?" the voice whispered again.

I was scratching my boots. Fidgeting. Making noise for the sake of noise, and action for the sake of action.

I still wore the dress from Pranish's party. Black as it may be, I saw darker patches, now crusty, where blood had splattered onto the material. Was some of that blood Colin's?

I scratched harder. And harder, until I rubbed the tip of my finger raw.

"Kat!" the voice shouted, waking me suddenly from my stupor.

"What?!" I shouted back, and I felt that I'd usually feel shame at the sound of my voice. It was choked, filled with tears I hadn't yet shed. And a guilt that I'd not shed them. Why wouldn't I cry? For Colin? Was I that inhuman? So jaded and cruel?

"Kat," Treth said, quieter now. "We have to do something. We have to start working on our escape."

"Colin's dead," I said, matter of factly.

I leant back. My hand stopped fidgeting, falling limply to my side.

"What's the use?" I said and felt both a pang of shame both from myself and from Treth.

"Andy…" Treth started.

"Don't you fucking say that name!" I yelled, sitting upright.

"Calm, Kat. Rage isn't going to get us out of here. And we need to get out of here if we're going to kill him."

Kill him. I'd promised him that. I had to do it. Andy was some sort of monster. A lycanthrope by the looks of it. How did I not realise it? In hindsight, I saw the signs. The predatory territorialism, his suspicious absences, and the fact that Oliver's eyes glowed yellow and he growled at me. We saw the signs. But didn't do anything about them. It wasn't even like werewolves were a protected species. While vampires were humans under the Spirit of the Law, werewolves were considered too bestial to have the same rights. I could have ended Andy as soon as I saw his eyes glow yellow. How would have Trudie treated me after that? Well, now it didn't matter. Colin was dead. I was too late. Now, all I could hope for was revenge.

"We'll need a silver blade," I said, my voice husky, cold, calculating. "An axe, maybe. For beheading. Or an executioner sword."

"First, we need to get out of this cell."

I looked around, as if noticing my confinement for the first time. It was not what I imagined the cell of a necromancer lord to look like. I looked at the bed behind me. I had been lying on it when I awoke but had promptly slumped onto the floor to brood. At the foot of the bed was a change of clothes. I sniffed. Besides the smell of lavender around me, I smelled sweat and blood. I needed a shower.

As if he read my mind, Treth spoke. "There seems to be a bathroom over there."

I felt rather than saw him point and turned my head. A glass door, adjacent to the solid metal side door. I opened it to reveal a small, yet functional bathroom. A toilet, basin and shower.

"Why?" I whispered. "Why all this?"

"The Marshal said that you're her greatest ally."

I glowered. "But why? And, more importantly, what does that mean for me?"

"I don't know, Kat. I really don't. But what I do know is that she's a necromancer. She's the enemy. We must do what we can to escape."

"And to kill that monster…"

The stickiness of my dress became unbearable and I started to undress. I sensed Treth disappear into his ethereal chamber and felt a regretful loneliness. I didn't want to be alone. Even now. Not alone with these thoughts and in the heart of the beast.

"Treth?" I called, even as I stood nude in the bathroom, the tap not on yet. My bandages had been removed and the flesh healed. I doubt by the necromancer herself. Healing magic and necromancy didn't tend to mix. Light magic couldn't be used in dark weylines.

"Yes, Kat?" Treth reappeared, that reassuring presence at the back of my mind.

"Your eyes are closed, aren't they?"

"Yes."

"Why?"

"Because…"

"Because what?"

"It doesn't matter. What do you need?"

I was embarrassed to say it, but if I couldn't speak plainly to Treth, who could I talk to?

"Can you stay with me? For now? Eyes closed, or not. I don't want to be alone."

"Of course, Kat. I can do that."

I showered, using the shampoo and soap provided. I was sceptical at first, but I recognised the brands. And if she aimed to do something to me, the necromancer would have done it already.

The clothing set out for me was a simple t-shirt, jeans and fresh pair of underwear and socks. They were my size. They fit perfectly. That disturbed me. I knew the Necrolord had been watching me, but how did she know everything right down to my clothing size?

"Did you see anything when I was out?" I asked, hushed. I didn't know if the Necrolord was listening in or not.

Treth shook his head. "This miasma affects me as much as you. I saw the girl with blonde hair loom over us as the horde of vampires and people slept. Then, darkness. Then, this cell."

The vampires. The people. I hadn't thought about them. The monsters were after me. Charlene Terhoff, that she-vamp bitch, wouldn't quit until I was drained dry. Just because I'd killed her lover. Well, didn't matter if I deserved it or not. What mattered is that I led them to my friends. I'd risked their lives – if not ended them. What if the vampires had hurt, or even killed, Pranish or Trudie?

"I hope the others are okay…" I whispered, perishing the thought that I had gotten my friends killed, and felt tears about to rise, but they didn't. How cold was I?

"Pranish has security. Puretide was probably on the way the second that the vampires entered the building. The vamps were probably still asleep when the hunters staked and beheaded them."

"I hope so."

And if my friends were dead, I would live with the guilt of leading to their murder. Forever.

I looked around the cell again. No real openings. Just a tiny ventilation grille near the ceiling. No windows. It was the same in the bathroom.

I sighed. I needed more information. And I needed to find a vulnerability. I wouldn't find it here. But that didn't mean there weren't any in this stronghold. And if the Necrolord fancied me a friend, she wouldn't contain me forever.

Before Treth or I could stop myself, I shouted.

"Necrolord! You have me now. And you agreed to meet. Time to fulfil your bargain."

"What are you doing, Kat?"

"Finding a vulnerability," I whispered.

But no reply came.

Was she not listening in? Or was she toying with me? Or…was this a test?

I decided to play her game.

"Evergreen," I shouted. "That's your name, isn't it?"

Silence. More silence. And then I heard footsteps outside the door. Sneakers on concrete. Metal grated and a small shutter opened in the door, revealing a face that I would have thought pretty. Almost fae-like, if not for knowing what she had done.

"You got pretty far," Evergreen said. She cocked her head, considering me. Her face impassive. "But how far? Did you find my first name?"

"I didn't get anywhere," I almost spat. I'm bad at hiding my feelings. "Drake did. The investigator. C. Evergreen, he told me. And now he's dead. Did you kill him?"

C. Evergreen bit her lip, and looked up, as if listening to a voice inside her own head.

"Did you?" I repeated.

"No," she answered, serious. "I did not. But I know who did."

"Who?" I asked, a bit too eagerly, as I made a beeline for the door. I winced as I felt some pain on my injured foot. It hadn't been healed fully, even now.

She backed away, just slightly, and smiled, showing all her teeth. She had bags under her hazel-coloured eyes. Many sleepless nights. Yet, I saw the evidence of make up on her face. As if she had wanted to look her best for this meeting.

"Calm, Kitty Kat. I'm not your enemy," she said.

"Don't call me that!" I said, repressing a shiver.

She pouted. "Why? It's cute."

"It's creepy. Who killed Drake?"

She frowned, but then her face straightened again. Back to business.

"My ex-employers do not like it when their assets…go rogue. When I planned my exodus, I had contingency plans. Your friend…did not."

"The Council? Did they kill him?"

"Not exactly, Kit…Kat. But a faction within the Council did. You have crossed paths with them before. Thrice, I believe."

I found that hard to believe.

"When? How?"

She shook her head.

"Tell me!" I growled.

"I will. But you have been quite rude."

"Rude? You're the one who put me in a cell!"

"Would you kill me if I let you go free?"

I didn't answer. We both knew that I would.

"The cell is for my and your protection. For now, my friend."

"Friend? Why do you say we're friends?"

She grinned, and I saw a glint in her eyes. A sparkle.

"Did the Marshal not tell you? You are the one to help me with my grand design. The one that will protect me. The one that will save me."

"I don't save necromancers," I said, coldly. "I kill them."

"Way to infiltrate the enemy, Kat." Treth rolled his eyes. He didn't expect any different, though. I'm a warrior, not a spy.

"Why?" she asked, simply, cocking her head again.

"Why?! Because they're...you're...monsters. You created that abomination. You killed countless people. And...and..."

"A necromancer killed your family?"

I stopped and looked at her through the slot in the door. She looked more adult-like and serious than before. I looked into her hazel eyes. Deeply, and I knew that while her body was that of a child's, she'd seen too much in too little time.

"Yes," I finally answered.

"Me too," she replied, voice raising in pitch and speed. A mad glint came to light up her eyes. "And that is why I found you. Because we share a common origin. Orphans of the darker arts. But that is where we depart. When you saw a monster, and you saw loss, I saw an opportunity. Through the arts that led to their deaths, I can bring them back. And the pain will be worth it in the end. I'll have them back. And when I do, you will see. You will see what we can do if we tame the darkness."

"You're insane!"

"Insane? Perhaps. Now, you haven't asked the one crucial question yet."

I walked away from the door and sat on the bed. I felt a sudden exhaustion from the girl's outburst.

What question? I somehow figured it out. Something so petty, yet so important.

"What's your name?"

She smiled, and I heard an innocent energy to her voice. "Candace. Candace Evergreen. You can call me Candy."

Chapter 3. On the hunt

The blade hissed as it touched pale flesh. The vampire screamed. Like an animal caught in a trap. No. Not at animal. Brett would have cared if it was an animal. Animals had feelings. Emotions. Instincts that resembled morals. Animals belonged in this world. Vampires did not. And while the screams of animals would have made Brett hesitate, the scream of the vampire, as Brett's silver-edged bowie knife dug into its flesh, only gave him a cold satisfaction. He sometimes wondered if it had been his training in the Corps that allowed him to revel in the almost-human sound. Or if it had been simply a by-product of what the monsters had done to him. It did not matter at the end of the day. What mattered was that he did not flinch at the screams. They only fuelled him.

56-3. His designation. His identity. It meant little to him now. Except for one thing. It had let him kill vampires. It had trained him. And with that skill, he'd save her.

Brett had arrived at the scene of Pranish's party after Puretide. Hammond had tipped him off. He'd been an asshole before but losing an arm had turned him into a cool guy. He was also worried about Kat. Worried enough that when he wasn't on an operation, he'd join Brett and Guy, scouring the city for the girl who'd saved his life. Hammond was working tonight. So was Guy. A drake had gotten into a penthouse apartment in Old Town. The MonsterSlayer App had come back online and, now, Drakenbane could do what it was built to do – kill drakes and their ilk. Brett called in sick. He had other work to do.

Vampires were sluggish during the day. Even when they were in the safety of the darkness, there was something about it being daytime that made them tired. Hesitant. They acted the same way humans did during the night. While the darkness held terror for humans, the day was just as terrifying to vampires. They knew how risky it was for them. That only a thin layer of clothing and a deceptively thick layer of concrete protected them from a light that would give them a death they'd worked so hard to avoid. Vampires feared the light, and Brett used that to full effect.

He had staked-out the bed-and-blood, a vamp twist on a bed-and-breakfast, the night before. Enough pale-skinned punks, dressed up like gothic posers, went in to pique Brett's interest. He made some calls, called in some favours and confirmed that the joint was a vamp hideout. In the day, he didn't knock.

A swift kick to the door brought it down. The vampire at the counter had been filling in a crossword ("Belarus" was the answer for 3-down). Brett eviscerated its face with silver pellets. He rushed the vamp as it tried to recover and cut off its head with a swift chop from a hand-axe. He didn't stop to listen. He kicked down the next door. The vamps weren't armed. This was a resting area. A form of barracks. They thought themselves safe. They thought they didn't need to sleep with a gun. That their curse would protect them. Brett loved to prove them wrong.

Those who resisted too vehemently were beheaded. The others were bound with silver-plated chains and then covered in trash-bags. He carried them out of the building, one by one, placing them in the back of his car. He hadn't blacked out the windows. If any vamp tried to get free, they'd get toasted. They'd feel the warmth of the sun on the plastic bags around their heads. They'd know what it meant. Brett wanted them to know what it meant.

He'd been put in a similar bag before. He had been subjected to the whispers. To the snarls. To the gloating. And then to the slurping, and gut-wrenching sounds of those around him being eaten alive. That had been long ago, but people never forgot something like that. It stuck with them. Forever. And only death could make one forget, if only for a little while.

Brett wanted the vamps to suffer. For them all to suffer. And then to die. But not before they told him where Kat was. For her, he was willing to slow his hatred. From a red-hot rage, to something colder. Machine-like. For Kat, he would speak to the monsters before putting them down.

Brett released the handle of the knife, still in the vampire's forehead. It wasn't deep. Just the tip, pointing into the vamp's brain. The vamp wasn't too much of a fledgling that his regeneration wouldn't be able to fix it once the silver was gone. Brett was counting on that. He needed all the information he could get. To do that, he needed to butter these vamps up. He needed to show them that while they forsook their humanity, they hadn't let go of pain. And Brett knew how to make a vampire feel pain.

The vamp looked up at him, with red, pleading eyes.

"Stop pretending to be human," Brett muttered, and flicked the hilt of the knife. The blade shook in the vamp's skull and it groaned in pain. It couldn't move his limbs, as its arms were chained to the ceiling, and its legs clamped to the ground.

Brett would keep the vamp like this until it expired. Or he didn't need the vamp anymore.

Some people would think Brett a monster for doing this. Some people already had called him one. Vampires were people, they said. They had rights. The Spirit of the Law protected them. They had human rights.

But they weren't human. They were monsters. And Brett hunted monsters.

Brett leant in close, giving the vampire the opportunity to see and smell his neck. The vampire groaned. Half in agony and half in lust. In pain, anticipation, hunger and pleasure.

Brett moved away and saw the disappointment in the vamp's eyes.

"The girl. Kat Drummond. Where is she?"

"I don't..." the vamp coughed up blood and continued, the knife bobbing in its head. "Fucking know, man. I'm from out of town. I don't know what the fuck you're talking about."

"That's unfortunate," Brett said. "Because there's only one reason I'd keep a creature like you alive..."

"I thought we weren't monsters here," the vamp shook its head, the knife shaking. He winced.

"You're always monsters."

Brett took out the knife, causing the vampire to cry out.

"Where is Kat Drummond?"

A bestial hiss caused Brett to turn, just as a vampire, ripped chains trailing from his arms, leapt at him from behind. A bolt found its mark in the vampire's head, going right through, and pinning the creature to the wall.

"I was using that," Brett said, and turned to the figure in the sunlit doorway. The chained-up vampire recoiled, as sunlight pooled just before it. Centimetres away from its bare feet.

"There are plenty of others," Conrad Khoi said, impassively. He held a hand crossbow facing the roof. He did not wear his typical salesmen suit get-up, instead opting for a leather trench coat. Brett inspected the bolt. Solid silver plating. The vampire's chest heaved. Slowly. Brett would still be able to interrogate it.

"It won't do you any good," Conrad said. "These are basically fledglings. They won't know anything. And it isn't even certain that vampires took her."

"You saw it?"

"The apartment? I saw vampire corpses. Human corpses. I saw Kat's boyfriend staining the bookshelf. I saw Puretide mucking everything up. And I didn't see Kat."

"They got her. I know they did. Blood Cartel, or Sanguineas. Or whatever outfit that Terhoff bitch is with. I will find her, Conrad. And I'll kill every single fucking blood-sucker in this city if that's what it takes."

Conrad nodded. "But why are you so certain that they took her?"

"I know vampires, demon hunter. And I know that you've grown soft. Flabby. The 90s were a long time ago. Your golden age of purging is done. Leave the hunting to the next generation."

"It's almost done." Conrad nodded. "But not yet. Not until we find Kat."

"Then, help me."

"When I can. But I have my own leads. Cindy and I are looking into the Digby connection," Conrad said, unmoving from the doorway.

"That crazy priest?" Brett replied, almost bored. He wanted to get back to the interrogation. The clock was ticking.

"Kat claimed that the archdemon turned on him. But that he had friends."

"Friends that would want to harm Kat?"

"Kat has made a lot of enemies."

"No thanks to you," Brett growled.

"This is our business, Brett. You know this all too well. She chose this life. Just as much as you did."

"We didn't choose this life," Brett grunted. "We were forced into it. By necessity. Because we knew that if not us, who?"

"Please...let me go. I have kids." The vampire rasped.

Brett planted the knife into the vampire's skull. Deeply. Too deeply. The creature died.

Conrad frowned at the man-creature, slumped over in its chains. Brett looked at him pointedly.

"We all have our own methods."

"Yes, yes we do."

Conrad turned to leave. Then stopped.

"I hired her for a reason, Corpsman. I won't let her die."

He continued walking, but Brett heard him whisper.

"I owe her that much, at least."

Chapter 4. Necromancy

The words hurt. They felt like sandpaper on my brain, smeared with acid. I wanted to vomit the first time I thought about them. I did heave when I said them. The spells failed. Each and every time. I cried. I spat. I drooled vomit and blood-drenched saliva. I beat at the body, long deceased and belonging to people with no loved ones or history, willing it to rise. The Mentor, the man with the reassuring hand on my back and voice in my ear, would only smile, encouragingly, and rub my head. He'd tell me to try again. I did. Again, and again. And I muscled through the pain. The knives in my head and the darkness that I so feared looming over me.

After retrieving my parents' corpses from the graveyard, where we could safely contain them without nosy neighbours and police, I came to live with the Mentor. I did not have a permanent home. Instead, I spent days in different places, all around the world. Johannesburg in the Goldfield Magocracy, in the mountains of the Scandinavian League, the husks of the Central USA, the islands of Polynesia, and the spider-torn wastelands of Australia. I wasn't told the location of some of the places we visited. The Mentor kept me away from people. He didn't want me to become distracted.

"You have important work to do," he would say, rubbing my head and giving me a reassuring smile. Sometimes, he would disappear for days, leaving me in our safehouse of the day, with an old man with grey hair named Robert, that he called Igor, despite the man not at all resembling a deformed hunchback. He was named after the servant of Dr Frankenstein in the films. Not the book. Mentor had insisted I read the book, among many others. I learnt that Frankenstein was the creator of the monster, and not the monster itself. I learnt of the notion of the modern Prometheus, and how humanity sought and seeks to depose God. I read this tale and found myself becoming simultaneously aghast by Frankenstein's hubris in attempting to take the role of God and mother in his creation of life, but also intrigued. And the more I repeated the darkly woven words, the less my head hurt, and the more I found that Frankenstein's problem was not hubris, but a lack of conviction. He had created a monster and shunned it. When he should have embraced it. Tamed it. The solution was not to deplore the darkness. It was to use it.

And as I came to realise this, the words inside my head became honey, and I wanted more, and more. They became a beautiful melody. Frankenstein's goals became petty to me. Selfish. But still intriguing. I'd use him as an inspiration. Not to create new life, but to bring back my parents. Until then, they would remain frozen, in the Mentor's stronghold in Hope City.

Even though the words became less and less painful as I repeated and memorised them, I still failed to raise the corpses that the Mentor provided me. It was not like the time I had used the magic of the man in black. Desperation had carried me then. The darkness embraced the desperate and I had embraced it in return. But now, I could not help but shove against it, despite knowing that I needed it to bring my parents back. But, was I good enough? Could I tame it? Could I control monsters?

The Mentor wasn't home. He had left a few hours ago, not saying where he was going. This was normal. I had lived with him for a year now. I spent more time with Igor than him, and while Igor was quiet most of the time, he had his own ways of showing his affections. Voiceless smiles. Hot tea. Practical shows of kindness. I liked him.

We were staying in a hot country. Not humid. And there was sometimes a refreshing breeze. It felt like Hope City, but the architecture was different. Shocking white houses, with flat roofs. They felt carved out of the rock. I was allowed outside, but the house was alone on a small island, surrounded by sea. There was a beach below the cliff, and I could feel the ocean breeze come through my open window. Sometimes, I swam in the water, but found myself bored of this quickly. Books were of much more interest to me than sandcastles and salt water.

I clutched my head and winced as my eyes glanced over scratchy symbols on a black leather-bound tome. Only some words no longer hurt but, after too much time, I would still get headaches.

I glanced up as I heard a clink of glass. Igor, showing his concern through a creased brow, placed a glass of ice-water on the table to my side.

"Thank you," I said, and tried to smile. But that made my head hurt more. I settled for a serious frown. He smiled anyway, and squeezed my shoulder, reassuringly.

I took a long sip of water. I got a brain freeze but it actually felt refreshing. Natural. I'd much rather have it than the toxic pain from the words. But I knew I needed that pain. To test me. To ensure I had what it took. Virtue was found through suffering. And the greatest virtue was taming the darkness. I had to earn it!

I left the now empty glass on the table and turned back to the tome. The Mentor had taught me how to read Grafscripp, the otherworldly language of necromancy, but I still had to squint to make out the seemingly incomprehensible scratchings on the paper. The Mentor had told me that this book wasn't from Earth. That it had been in the possession of a necromancer from Stradgorf who had been dragged onto our planet. He called it, *The First Books*. The founding texts of his kind on Earth. The fact that he let me read it, especially read it without his supervision, made me feel warm. He trusted me, and I felt I needed to earn that trust again and again. I needed to revive my parents, but I also came to desire pleasing the Mentor. Just to hear his rare affirmations, I became willing to do anything.

"How is the studying, mistress?" Igor asked, as he retrieved the glass.

"I don't know, Igor. I feel it in my head, but nothing happens. Not like before." I shook my head. "I hope

Mentor isn't disappointed. And I hope I can finally do as he asks."

"You will," Igor replied, warmly. "The master has patience. And he knows that this is a delicate craft. It requires years of practice and rare talent."

"But what if I don't have that talent?"

"Then the master would not have accepted you in the first place." Igor winked. "The master doesn't make mistakes."

Doesn't make mistakes.

I tightened my fists, with a newfound determination. I had to prove myself. The Mentor didn't make mistakes. I wouldn't be his first.

I read the symbols, even as the sun went down and the sky darkened. Igor offered to turn on a light, but I didn't answer. He did not switch the light on. I think he knew. These words of darkness performed best in the shadows. They sprang out of the page and became alive. They more easily nestled inside my head, becoming acquainted with my psyche, and my psyche with them. I read more and more, until I finished the tome, and I didn't understand why I had struggled to read it in the first place. The words no longer hurt at all.

"Igor," I called, calmly, but I felt a rasp in my throat. Yet, my throat wasn't dry, and I did not feel sick or tired.

"Yes, mistress?"

"I would like to attempt a reanimation," I said.

"Now?"

I nodded.

"Are you sure, mistress? The master will be back soon. He would be able to provide proper supervision."

"Do I need supervision?" I hissed and was surprised by the venom in my own voice.

There was a tense pause. Igor bowed his head.

"Of course not. I shall prepare the body."

"Do that," I said, my mind half somewhere else. I heard clicks and fumbling as Igor retrieved the body from cold-storage and carried it to the ritual area. I stood up from my study-desk, the night now truly dark, and my eyes attuned to the shadows. I cracked my back and made my way down the stairway, towards the ritual area. In the past, I had felt nervous whenever I had taken these steps, at whatever house, to the almost always subterranean or roof-top ritual area. In this house, the ritual area was located below the surface, submerged below the island. The walk to the ritual area, with or without the Mentor, was always ominous. I had never succeeded in incanting words of darkness after my experience with the man in black. All these long walks ever culminated in was failure and embarrassment. But now, I felt different. With or without the Mentor at my back, I would succeed now. I knew it.

The ritual room was circular. A small dome, with a stone-floor, spiderwebbed with intricate patterns and grooves dug into the floor, meant to carry blood like the canals in Venice did water. In the centre of the room was a stone tablet. Igor stood to the side of the tablet, rubbing his back. He was not a young man anymore and carrying the deadweight of a frozen corpse was not an activity I envied. The corpse in question was that of a middle-aged man with chestnut hair. His eyes were closed, and his hands were clasped on his chest as he lay naked on the stone tablet. I had been embarrassed by the nudity of these corpses in the past but had long since become used to it. It was not like seeing a living man nude. It was like a doll. A toy. One did not feel uncomfortable due to the nudity of a mannequin.

"Is everything ready, Igor?" I asked.

"Mistress? Your voice…it sounds different."

"I am different. I think…I know I have grasped the darkness. I will succeed now."

Igor nodded, and backed away, behind me. He stood at attention, hands clasped behind his back.

"Will you need the tome?"

"No, Igor. I have what I need."

I moved forward, and touched the feet, hands and forehead of the corpse. He was thawing fast in the evening heat. I committed the man's face to memory. He looked about my father's age.

I closed my eyes, and pictured the scratchy Grafscripp, until the words became real, and I opened my eyes and saw them floating around my head.

I spoke a word as it passed into view and felt bile rise. I willed my body to obey. To resist the urge to vomit out the taint. The word stuck on the tip of my tongue, like it was caught in traffic. Congested, claustrophobic, and unable to move or breathe. The bile rose but caught in my throat. The word still did not come. There was still something stopping it.

I had not truly embraced the darkness, yet.

And I thought of my family. My mother nailed to the roof. My father, dying in and of pure pain. I thought of how I had killed their murderer. With the darkness.

I needed to be desperate. But not so desperate that I let the darkness control me.

I needed to make a deal.

I give you everything. I told myself, and the darkness at the periphery of my soul. *I give you everything for the power I need. Everything but my soul.*

I felt the darkness ponder my offer. The bile felt like acid in my throat and the word on the tip of my tongue starved me of oxygen.

The darkness nodded, as if it could nod. And disappeared. The bile dispersed, and the word escaped my lips. It tasted and sounded first like magma, and then ambrosia.

I felt an immense power surging through my chest and loins. Power to do anything. To save my parents. Eventually.

I said the next word. And the next. And every word filled me with unexplainable pleasure. I felt the weyline flow through my soul and out my fingertips, as dark green light and smoky tendrils grasped at the man, infesting his pores.

He twitched, and I almost giggled in delight. I was doing it! I was really doing it. All this effort. All this time. All this suffering. I was raising the dead!

The Mentor had not failed. I had not failed him.

My incantation ceased. The corpse did not move. I felt a stab of pain in my gut. Was I wrong? Did I mess something up? But I was so close!

And then the corpse's eyes opened, suddenly. They were milky-white.

"You did it, mistress!" Igor exclaimed, his excitement palpable.

I didn't reply. My satisfaction held me still as the man I had raised from the grave orientated himself, staggering off the metal slab.

I had brought life to the lifeless. I was now a necromancer. And it was only a matter of time before I saved my parents from their untimely deaths.

The corpse shivered as it stood, and slowly panned its head across the room.

"What are you going to call your first servant?" Igor asked.

I didn't reply. The living corpse looked at me, and then at Igor. Through our necromantic connection, I felt its intent.

I whispered, with as much authority as I could muster. "No."

I felt its voiceless reply loudly. "Yes."

The corpse shuffled past me, and I turned.

"Stop!" I shouted.

"Mistress?" Igor asked, incredulous.

"Run, Igor!"

Igor looked confused but, as the zombie staggered closer, his speed improving as his body thawed, the truth dawned. Igor paled with fright and made a dash for the stairway. The zombie let out an unnaturally deep snarl and leapt.

I imagined myself tackling the zombie to the ground. I imagined beating it and saving my friend. But I was not a fighter. I was a young girl, with books and magic powers. I could only imagine saving Igor, even as the zombie chewed into his leg, pulled him down, Igor screaming for me to save him. The zombie bit into his neck, silencing his screams. Blood sprayed like a fountain. And stopped.

I only felt the pain in my hand when it started to bleed. I had been biting into it. I felt tears threatening to well up, but none came. I only watched as Igor was torn to shreds by my creation.

Hubris.

The modern Prometheus. Chained to a rock to face his sins for eternity. Yet, like Frankenstein, my punishment was the sin itself.

This is what happened when we played God.

Igor no longer resembled a human as I heard footsteps slowly descend the steps. The zombie arched its head up. The Mentor looked back at the corpse, unflinching. The zombie charged him even as I put in all my will for it to stop. Before my eyes, the zombie fell limp. A corpse again.

I collapsed to my knees.

"I'm sorry, master! I'm so sorry. I thought I could control it. I didn't know it would do that. I'm so sorry."

The Mentor charged me, and I flinched, even as he caught me in his arms and squeezed me tightly, laughing.

"I knew you could do it! This is the first step. You have tamed the darkness. You are an amazing student."

The words calmed me even as I saw Igor's bloodied mulch and bones on the floor. I felt a warmth in my chest and a pang in my heart.

I had done it. I'd started my journey in earnest. And if that meant Igor had to die, then it was a small price to pay for the happiness I now felt in Mentor's arms.

Chapter 5. Beauty

I awoke in the cell bed, the day after my discussion with Candace – or Candy. I had struggled to fall asleep as my situation dawned on me and I continued to remember Colin's final moments. When that became too unbearable, I pondered what had happened to my friends. I pondered what would happen to me. The latter was the least offensive of all my thoughts. I'd faced death many times before. But losing Colin…

Finally, my exhaustion caught up with me, and I slept. Mercifully, I did not remember my dreams in the morning. But I did wake up in a cold sweat, my heart pounding, and feeling an intense guilt that I could not explain.

"Awake?" Treth asked. I opened my eyes and nodded.

"Good. We should start planning our escape."

"I agree," I whispered back, glad that he was shifting my thoughts to something else. "But, there's something else…"

"What?"

"She knows stuff. We need to find out more."

"That assumes she can be trusted," Treth replied.

"It's odd…"

"Yes, it is."

"I mean…trusting her is odd. She's a necromancer, and mad, but…"

"But nothing," Treth butted in. "She's embraced the darkness. We get out. We kill Andy. We kill her. The order doesn't matter. As long as both die."

I normally would have nodded, but something stopped me.

"I don't think it's that simple. And despite her madness, despite the darkness…I don't think she's lying to us."

"Why?" Treth sounded incredulous, and just a little accusatory.

"We suspected the Council already. And what would she have to gain by lying about her involvement with them?"

"She wants you to serve her. She's said it quite openly. She wants you to trust her, in order to serve her…"

"You know that won't happen. I don't serve anyone. Much less a necromancer…"

Treth paused, and then whispered, even though only I could hear him. "I'm sorry, Kat. It's just…you know my past. What happened to my brother. When darkness beckons, few reject its call. I trust you, Kat. I love you. But I also loved my brother. And he embraced the darkness."

"Love?" I asked, just as I heard another voice on the outside of the metal cell door.

"Who are you talking to?" Candace asked quietly, voice muffled by the cell door. I didn't hear her approach. She must have been standing by the door since I woke up. Very creepy. But, in a way, somewhat sad. That she would spend so long, idle by a cell door, waiting for someone else alive to speak to.

"I have the spirit of a knight from another realm living inside my head," I answered, truthfully. Typically, people thought I was just being sarcastic when I gave them this answer.

"Cool! Is he dead? What realm is he from? How long have you had him? What's his name? Wait…is it a him?"

Candace believed me.

"Good job, Kat…" Treth moaned, now the one to be sarcastic.

"Does it really matter if she knows about you?" I answered, out loud.

"What did he say?" Candace asked, her voice filled with childish excitement.

"Don't tell her," Treth grumbled.

"He thinks I shouldn't have told you about him."

"So, it is a him?" Her tone suggested a mischievous grin. "What's his name?"

I waited for Treth's consent, even if I hadn't before. He rolled his eyes. "Too late now."

"His name is Treth. He's from Avathor."

"The dead world?"

I felt Treth wince.

"I don't know. He doesn't like to talk about it."

Silence.

"I'm sorry, Treth," Candace said, sounding embarrassed.

"Sorry for what?" he replied, as if speaking directly to her. I repeated his words.

"Reading about the dead worlds," she began, sounding sad. "And knowing they are and were real is very different. I was insensitive."

Treth didn't reply. I felt his shock. I was also shocked. Too often I had thought of necromancers as comparable to the monsters they created. I forgot that they were human, with human embarrassment and, it seemed, human sympathy.

"Kat?" Candace asked.

"What?"

"If I let you two out, will you kill me?"

I considered the question. Would I? I'd made an oath that I would. Necromancers were the enemy. Human or not. For all that she had done and would do, she needed to die. But…I needed to leave this cell.

"I won't kill you if you let me leave this cell."

I didn't know if I was lying or not.

"Promise?"

I hesitated. I just had to lie. To bide my time. It was so simple. But, why then did the words become so hard to say?

"I promise."

"Pinky-swear?"

"What?" I didn't know what else to say to that.

"Pinky-swear!" she said, excited. I heard her stand up. She had been leaning up against the cell door, sitting on the floor. She opened the shutter and put her hand through. A small, pale hand, with fingernails cut and filed for practical work.

"What is pinky-swearing?" Treth asked. "Is it some sort of binding ritual?"

"You could say that," I said, incredulous. "But not magical."

"Then do it," he said. "Then we slay her."

I got off the bed and made my way to Candace's eager hand peeking through the shutter.

I stopped, just in front of the door, and took a deep breath. I gripped Candace's pinky with mine. Her hand was callused, yet I felt a youthful softness underneath. She let go and withdrew her hand. I heard clicks, and the door slid open on screeching rails.

Candace was quite a bit shorter than me, the top of her head only coming up to my chin. She wore a black robe that reached down to her thighs. Blue jeans below. She wore white sneakers, and had a pink hairclip, keeping her blonde bangs out of her eyes.

At that moment, I considered killing her. It would be easy. Easier than a zombie. I could reach my hands out and place them around her throat. I wouldn't even need to wait for her breath to leave her. I could snap her fragile, young neck before she could utter a single corruption incantation. I could kill her, and my oath would be completed. Another monster dead.

But, was she a monster?

63

With her eager eyes, looking up at me like I was a long-lost big sister. With her innocent smile. And with the blood smattered on her white shoes…

I didn't raise my hands. I only passed the threshold, into a dark, concrete hallway, with tile floors and a flickering lightbulb. There were doorways like this one to my left and right, with an unnatural darkness just past them. I felt an intense uneasiness at the darkness, that stopped me seeing further than I should have. Just like the stronghold where Hammond had lost his arm.

Treth didn't tell me to kill her. Either because he wanted me to bide my time, or because, like me, he started to see the humanity in this little girl. But it wasn't just that for me. As I saw her, bouncing on her heels, unable to keep still, I was curious about this monster in human form.

"This can still be your room, but I will have a lock installed so you can enter or exit as you like. You now have full permission to explore the stronghold. But I cannot allow you to leave."

"Like Beauty and the Beast?" I muttered, trying to peer through the darkness.

"Which are you?" Candace asked, grinning.

I frowned. "Um…the Beauty."

"Oh." She looked disappointed, and them moved so I could press further into the hall. She began walking, and I followed.

"The stronghold is large," Candace began. "So, make sure to note where you are. It isn't dangerous if you get lost, but the darkness will make it hard to find your way back."

I jumped as we walked past a flesh-puppet, standing still as a statue. He wore the armour of a riot policeman.

"The undead will not harm you. I do not keep zombies within this level of the stronghold. Only flesh-puppets."

I leaned in closer to examine the flesh-puppet. He showed no recognition.

"How do you maintain so many of them? Without your wight, especially."

"The Marshal? He never controlled any of the flesh-puppets. Only I did."

"How?" I couldn't help but sound and be awed. Necromancers were my enemies, but I knew a bit about their systems. Controlling this many flesh-puppets...it would require immense power and immense skill. Who was Candace? And how did she get to this point in her life? How was she so powerful yet so young?

I turned to face her, and came face to face with a dirty, yellow-tinted creature, with black dreaded hair and crazy yellow eyes. I jumped back, reaching for swords that weren't there.

The creature giggled, and I remembered where I had heard that sound before. The stronghold. It seemed a lifetime ago.

"What is that thing?" I asked, unable to keep my nerves out of my voice.

"She's not a thing," Candace replied, sounding offended. "She's Petunia. I made her."

"Made her? You mean reanimated."

The thing – Petunia – cocked its head, as if trying to understand what we were saying. Evidently bored, it scurried into the darkness, hunched over and touching the ground with its hands, as if a feral beast.

"No, Kat," Candace said, and continued walking. I followed, fast. Necromancer or not, I didn't want to be alone in these halls.

"Petunia is alive. Not dead. She is crafted from flesh-matter and organs, so is technically human, but was given the spark of life."

"Impossible. Necromancy doesn't deal in life. It twists death. Nothing else."

"Simplistic," she said, sounding more like an academic now than a child. "Necromancy, like any science, takes many forms. Death, life. Just two sides of the same coin. With a new perspective, the purpose of a tool can be changed. I have changed it. And I have created new life. A homunculus, a Frankenstein's monster. And in doing so, I have become a modern Prometheus."

I paused. Dumbstruck. "How old are you again?"

"14. Why?"

"You know an awful lot for a 14-year-old."

"I read," she said, as she turned down the corner of the hallway. Suddenly, the darkness abated, revealing a well-lit apartment, adorned with a couch, armchair, kitchenette, bookshelf, and a door leading to another room, with a sign reading: "Candy <3"

It looked…normal. Not the twisted abode of a necromancer, the penthouse of a gang leader or the squalid bunker of a criminal in hiding. It looked like any normal, albeit small, apartment. It could have easily been mine – if not for the lack of windows.

"I'll keep a look out for a place to escape," Treth said.

"What did he say?" Candace asked, curious and excited.

"What makes you think he spoke?"

"You look up, as if contemplating the ceiling, whenever he speaks," she said.

Well, fuck. And here I was thinking I had everything covered up.

"Do you live alone?" I asked, trying to change the topic.

"No...and yes. I have my servants. But they aren't exactly *living* with me."

"Unliving, then." I grinned, unable to contain myself.

"Was that a pun?"

I didn't reply.

Candace turned her back to me, but I saw a hint of a smile. She made her way to the counter of the kitchenette and turned on an electric kettle.

"Tea? Coffee?"

"Don't take anything. It could be a trap," Treth said.

That was stupid. I'd already eaten her food last night. If she wanted to mindwarp or mutate me, she had every opportunity already.

"Coffee, please."

"Black?"

"Yes."

"I prefer tea," she said. "Rooibos. With honey. Ironic, isn't it?"

"What is?"

"You, a servant of light, drinking black coffee. Me, a necromancer, who likes sweet tea."

"Humans are too complex to analyse based on their beverages."

"On the contrary, Kat. I believe you can tell a lot about someone by what they prefer to drink."

She poured the hot water into the respective mugs and prepared the drinks, while I stood awkwardly to the side. Finally, she indicated the couch and armchair and I followed as she placed the drinks on the coffee table.

She closed her eyes as she drank. Looking serene. I drank my coffee, a bit sceptical of its safety due to Treth's paranoia. But it tasted normal, if badly made. Bitter. If I could be judged by what I drank, did that mean I was bitter? Like black coffee. Nothing but caffeine, heat and cynicism.

"Coffee is complex, I've read," Candace said, eyes still closed. "If left too long to stew, it comes out bitter and acrid. But if fresh, and prepared well, it is filled with a medley of complex flavours."

She opened her eyes.

"What does that say about you, Kat?"

"That I don't really care about the taste of what I drink."

I took a long sip and placed the mug on the table.

"If you're going to spend time with her, at least try to get some information," Treth hissed. He didn't like this.

"Yesterday, you started to speak about the Council. How you worked for them. You also mentioned that I have encountered…a part of the Council…"

"Three times," she finished my sentence. She placed her mug down on the coffee table and held up a single finger.

"First time. Jeremiah Cox. Necromancer. Called himself The Purity."

I remembered him all too well. Sometimes, I still felt his blood on my hands.

"He was funded by a group that calls themselves the Conclave. Reason? From what I gathered: he was a destabilising element. A decoy, if you will. He helped cover up something that the Conclave wanted covered up. You know? False-flags, red herrings. What is a few hundred dead if it keeps something else out of the news?"

"But it was you who led me to his lair at North Road, wasn't it?"

"Yes. And that seems like an age ago. Before I had my local holdings. I have grown a lot since then."

I tensed my fists and had to speak through gritted teeth.

"You used your dark magic on me."

"I had to, Kat," she pleaded. "You had swords. You were going to kill me. Would you have let me survive if you knew that I was a necromancer?"

"Back then? Probably. It was Jeremiah who popped my cherry."

"Gross."

"Go on. My second encounter with this...Conclave?"

"The Blood Cartel. Vampires set on destroying the city and the world with the help of their dark god. The Conclave helped them. I was hired to aid in their pursuits."

"You helped them kill a lot of people."

She shrugged. "A means."

I almost stood up, enraged, but calmed myself.

"The Blood Cartel," she continued. "Was aided by the Conclave. To what end, I do not know. But if the Blood Cartel's goal was destruction, then it is safe to assume that

71

the Conclave would have benefited from this destruction in some way."

She raised three fingers in total.

"Cornelius Black and Joshua Digby. Christians convinced that they needed to bring on the second coming with fire and death. Ultimate goal: awakening the Titan Under the Mountain. Also enabled by the Conclave."

"I heard him speak to someone on the phone. Before he was killed."

"You didn't kill him?"

I shook my head. "A demon did."

"Demons are fickle. Not like my servants."

She looked at her lap. Her fingers twitched. "Or perhaps similar, in some circumstances."

"Why did you work for this Conclave?" I finally asked. "Did you agree with their goals of total destruction?"

She shook her head. "I never cared what they wanted. For me, it was about what my mentor told me to do, and that was only for one reason."

She looked at me more sternly, and I saw the twinkle of lucidity in her eyes.

"You told the Marshal that you do not accept death. Neither do I. I do what I do to see my parents again. To bring them back."

"As wights?"

"No. The way they were. The way I remember them. Living. Breathing. And so, I can tell them sorry. For everything I didn't say sorry for before, and everything I have done since then."

"Necromancy can't return life, Candace." I shook my head, as if lecturing a child. But could I really consider her a child? "It can only imitate. Twist death into a facade. Necromancy provides the charade, but they wouldn't be your parents."

"No, Kat. You are wrong. That is what the darkness wants us to believe. But I've seen the truth. The darkness can be tamed. It can be used for good. And I can bring back my parents with it. And it'll all be worth it. Worth the head-screaming. The aching-aches. It'll be worth becoming…becoming…like…like HIM. The darkness beckons me, Kat. But I'll show it. I'll show all of it. And you. We will all be together with them again."

She had been shouting, but stopped, suddenly. Lucidity returned to her madness-hazed eyes, and she rubbed her head.

"The pain means I can see," she muttered. "I can see past it. The pain is good. Not the sweetness."

She glanced at me, suddenly. I felt Treth recoil as I considered doing so.

"I hope you understand," she said, in almost a whisper. "The Conclave is after you. And it is after me. It thought that we would kill each other. But its wrong. He's wrong. Now, we can protect each other."

She stood up and made her way to the kitchenette, as I tried to come to terms with what she had said.

"What would you like for dinner?" she asked.

"Ramen," I replied, without hesitation, even as I scratched at my jeans, not knowing my next move.

Chapter 6. The Corps

Vampire blood wasn't corrosive, but it held its own dangers. A speck ingested could create an addict. Addicts became customers. Customers became thralls. Thralls kept the vampires fed and powerful. A powerful vampire was dangerous. And Brett knew all too well how dangerous a vampire could become.

In his Corps days, only a kid, he had been sent into a small town by the Limpopo/Gauteng border. One-horse town. A gas-station with a shop, a church, some houses and a tiny school. Nothing fancy. Brett had grown up in Johannesburg under the Magocracy Magnates. He knew what a city looked like. A real city. It stretched further than the eye could see. It had more people than anyone could genuinely count. And it held secrets. Far too many secrets.

This town had no secrets. Not anymore. Its people were strewn across the streets, blood drained from their bodies, missing limbs. Some had visible damage around their genitalia. Others had their breasts ripped right off. Almost all the corpses were naked. None of them facing ghoulification. The vampires had been in too much of a hurry to drain their victims dry. They only fed until death, and then moved on to the next victim. And the next. And the next.

No one had survived, except for a trucker with an affinity for pyromancy. He had managed to keep the blood-suckers back as he drove away to the nearest town, where the police were called, and then the army, and then...

"Extermination Corps!"

Brett turned to his commanding officer. The Corps ranks were simple. You got a number. Whoever was closer to 0 would be the commanding officer. Every tenth person in the section would be a corporal and have command over ten people. This was a fresh unit. 0 was still alive. That made him the manager. Brett was 56. That meant that 56 people needed to die before he was manager. By then, he would have 4 other people to command. As if it would matter at that point.

"Six groups of 10. Corporals, make sure the newbies don't get bit too quickly. Remember. Silver-shot first. Incapacitate them. Secure the area. Then, behead them."

The manager turned to his squad, and stopped, recalling an after-thought.

"Remember, they aren't human. They aren't even animals. Don't let their screams trick you. You give them any sorta mercy, and you'll die. And if you die bit by a fucking vamp, then you've failed the Corps. And if you fail the Corps, I'll bring you back from the fucking dead and kill you again myself. Now, move out!"

Brett trotted to his squad. His corporal was only a year older than he was. At the tail-end of the section, the oldest member was only 17. Brett thought that 17 was old. He was 15.

"Shoulder that shotgun, newbie!" the corporal shouted as Brett fell in line. Brett hastily tried to swing his shotgun on its straps but fumbled. 53, the 17-year-old, grabbed at the strap and took the shotgun in his hands. He passed it to Brett, who shouldered it the way he had briefly been trained. Very briefly. Only a month. A month, to learn how to slay vampires.

"We've got the outskirts of town," the corporal said, reading from a phone. It was not a normal phone. It could only be used to call other Corps phones. No outside contact was allowed. Too much to lose. The world didn't understand the importance of what they were doing, so they had to keep things secret. So, no phones. No letters. No family. It helped that almost everyone in the Corps had no family left. Brett wouldn't be in the Corps if he had. He wouldn't need to have joined. But now, he had no other choice.

He pumped his shotgun and inserted a cartridge full of silver-shot, and then another. He filled it to capacity and chambered a round.

"Ready, ladies?" the corporal tried to smirk, failed. Brett saw his hand shaking. The air wasn't cold.

Nobody answered. The corporal turned, and his group followed. The side-streets along the main road held similar scenes to the last. Corpses, broken doors, blood. Everywhere. Blood. The vampires wasted their meals. Decadent. Violent. Monsters.

"We sacrifice everything," 52 muttered, under his breath. "To avenge the fallen. To purify the world. Of the monsters and the demons."

He muttered the first few lines again, as if a stuck record. The Corps Oath. The group arrived at the outskirts of town, staring out onto empty fields and farmland in the distance, and a lone church, jutting out like a sore from the small town. Even from afar, Brett and the others could see the trail of blood and guts leading into the church. The doors were closed.

52 repeated the first part of the oath, again. 53 stopped him, placing his hand on his shoulder.

"Never forget," 53 continued the oath, "Earth is ours. And we will retake our world."

"The darkness holds no terror," Brett continued. "That the light cannot purify."

"And the Corps will outlast the end of the world," the corporal concluded.

He pointed at the church. "There's vengeance to be had in there, my brothers."

"We should phone in reinforcements. Ten isn't enough," 53 commented.

"Ten Corpsmen is more than enough for some vamp punks who thought they could ravage humanity," the corporal responded. He drew a machete. Its black metal contrasted with a shining layer of silver at its edge.

"We're tail-end of the section, corporal," 53 added. "We don't even have a purification sigil between any of us."

"You afraid, 53?"

"No…no, sir." 53 stammered out. Brett knew why 53's age hadn't made him corporal in the section. The Corps required guts. Killing monsters required guts. 53 was smart. He knew how to survive. But he didn't have what it took to reclaim Earth.

"Then, get back in formation. We're storming that church. Glory and vengeance will be ours."

"Yes, sir."

The group moved up towards the church, jumping over a waist-high fence even though the gate was open. Just to show that they could. When playing armies, you took the hardest route to prove that you could. Brett hadn't thought he was playing armies then. He thought he knew what he was getting himself into. He thought he had seen the worst that a vampire could do…

The river of blood led up the sandy hill towards the stone steps to the white church and its wooden door. Some bloody-handprints contrasted sharply with the clean white of the building. An overhang over the entrance provided some shade. Brett shivered. He had been taught to fear the shade. But to also go into it. To destroy the darkness, one had to enter it.

The corporal signed to the group to take positions by the door. The vamps, if there were any, had likely already heard them, but it was always best to get into an advantageous formation and breach according to the book.

Brett was near the front. 55, with an axe and silver stake, would open the door. Brett would enter first, firing at any enemies. This would be his first time in combat. His heart pounded harder than his shotgun would. But he had no inkling of turning back. Of retreating. His future, he was certain, was past this door.

Everyone in position. The corporal tapped 55 on the back. He opened the door. Brett, holding his breath, entered, shotgun first. As Brett breathed again, he wanted to vomit. Excrement, rot, blood, iron, urine, alcohol and tobacco all blended into a storm of stench that washed over them. Brett tried not to breathe it in as he proceeded further into the church, his compatriots behind him. He heard a crunch and aimed his shotgun into the dark. Some sunlight peaked through the boarded-up windows, illuminating a rat, carrying a finger in its mouth. Brett would have breathed a sigh of relief if it didn't mean inhaling the stench.

Some of the group turned on their flash-lights, creating tight beams of light that lit up the pews, ripped up psalm books, and desiccated corpses, their mouths frozen in terror. Some were missing eyes. Brett activated his flash-light, mounted on the side of the shotgun, realising it should have been on as he entered. He aimed the gun at the end of the church. Above the pulpit, nailed over a wooden crucifix and Christ, was a man wearing the black and white of a priest. Red stained the white, and dripped slowly, so slowly, into a brass collection plate below. Dripping. Tap. Tap. Tap. Tap. Tap…

It stopped. Brett heard clicks and the shuffle of feet as the group orientated towards the pulpit. Their flashlights struggled to penetrate the darkness, but even then, they saw it. Pulsating in the dark. Hunched over and writhing in what seemed to be dark smoke.

They heard a gut-wrenching slurp, and Brett heard one of them gag, even as they approached and levelled their weapons.

The slurping stopped, and they heard the plate return to its table-top. Tap. Tap. Tap.

"Fire," the corporal whispered.

Brett froze, trying to understand what he saw. A shadow. A hunched shadow. It looked like the darkness itself.

"Fire!" the corporal shouted.

Brett fired. The darkness didn't react. No cries. No thuds. The bang sounded, and the muzzle flared. The shot hit something. But past that – nothing.

"Veelas mo'galai…" a voice spoke, its voice sounding smooth. Melodic even. No guttural intonations. It sounded like honey. Yet, it filled Brett with dread.

He fired again. Pumped. Fired again. The room flashed with every shot. Others in the group fired their guns. Nothing. No reaction.

Tap. Tap. Tap.

Stopped. Slurping.

"Ffff…fall…" the corporal started to stammer. He was stopped as the creature spoke again.

"Your tongue…" it bellowed, rolling the final syllable in a deep rumble that came out as a menacing growl. "Is crude, but…I…will speak it to you, in your final…moments."

"Fall ba…!" the corporal's words stopped, and Brett heard gargling. The corporal shot forward, pulled by a black tendril, towards the black morass at the pulpit.

They heard gulping, sucking, and bone crunching. None of them moved. They couldn't. Something froze them to the spot. Fear, or some sort of incantation.

"The blood of...holy men," the creature continued, after finishing its meal. "Is said to be...tastier than any others. It must be consumed...delicately. But you..."

51 cried out, as he was pulled into the darkness. Brett tried to fire again, but he only heard clicks between the crunching, screaming, and splattering. He reached for his bandolier. He was knocked to the floor as 53 was pulled from behind him, screaming. Brett grabbed onto 53's arm. Saw the fear in his eyes. Blood dripped from his thigh, pooling onto the floorboards. The black tendril protruded from him, into the dark. The sounds of consumptions hadn't stopped. That explained why 53 was still clutching Brett's arm. When the slurping stopped, he would be dragged into the darkness. And whoever was with him.

There were no more screams from the dark. The feeding would stop soon. Brett looked into 53's pleading eyes. He bit into his own lip so hard that he made himself bleed.

The gulping and crunching stopped. Brett let go.

Tears welled up in Brett's eyes, even as he looked away from 53, being dragged into the darkness, and began to load his shotgun.

The tendrils shot out. More and more. Some of Brett's brothers managed to dodge. Others weren't so lucky. Brett lay on the ground. His shotgun was loaded, but what was the use?

He heard shouts from outside. They had to be here to help. More Corpsmen came running in. The tendrils skewered them, and the crunches and drinking rose in volume. The darkness rose larger and larger. Gunfire did nothing to it. Those who tried to charge it, found themselves skewered and eviscerated before they could cross two rows of pews. Brett managed to crawl, just far enough to hide under the pew. His heart threatened to beat out of his chest, and he panted hard, despite the stench in the room.

"For the Corps!" he heard a shout from one of the older members. It gave him some semblance of hope, but then the voice spluttered and screamed.

Silence fell on the church. Brett tried to stop his panting. To stay his breathing. Nobody else was left. Just him. He knew he was going to die. He rolled onto his back and held his shotgun upwards. Above him, looming over like a tidal wave frozen over the coast, was a creature with a pallid face, twisted with fangs and covered with blood.

Its body was black. Like a cloak that blended into its flesh and the shadows.

"Little...Corpsmen. Do you know what I am?"

Brett gulped, but found his words. "A monster."

The creature laughed. "Yes...a monster. And do you know what monsters do?"

Brett fired as way of answer. The pellet hit the pallid face and then fell to the ground. No trace of a wound.

"Monsters...exist in the shadows, my little Corpsman. Everywhere. Under your bed. In your closet. And in the hearts of your family. Your friends. Your entire life is filled with monsters."

Brett fired, and the creature smacked the shotgun out of his hands. It lifted Brett up, almost gently, with two tendrils grasping his arms.

"Monsters persist...little Corpsman."

It opened its mouth in a grimace, revealing shining white teeth between bits of sinew and gore.

"And most of all...monsters feed."

The creature moved its head towards Brett's neck just as they both heard the rumble of engines, the whirr of a rotor and the chopping of air. The building lurched. The creature dropped Brett to the ground as they heard rumblings, cracking, and the structure give. The rudimentary boards on the windows fell, releasing sunlight into the building. The creature hissed as the sun hit portions of its shadow. Those portions went up in smoke, releasing a sickly-sweet stench.

Slowly, with the semblance of an earthquake, the walls cracked and rose. Higher, higher. And then…the roof and the greater part of the walls were ripped from their foundations, allowing light to pool into the church, illuminating piles of dead, pools of blood, and a screaming monster that attempted to cover its eyes with its arms, even as its arms blistered and went up in fire and smoke. Brett watched as minutes passed, and the monstrous creature shrunk, screeching in pain, until it was no more than a pile of ash. He learnt to love that sound. And more than that, the sound of helicopter blades. A group of them, bearing no symbols. For the Corps did not need a symbol. Only a purpose. To slay monsters, and to outlast the end of the world.

***

But the Corps was gone.

Brett hadn't thought about them for years. Not since coming to Hope City. He thought he had put that all behind him. Too many comrades dead. And a purpose that blurred into genocide. Brett had not missed the Extermination Corps. Until now. For it was vampires that brought him into the Corps, and it was vampires that reminded him of everything else.

Brett was cleaning the blood off his weapons and strip-cleaning his guns when he heard a knock on his door.

"Guy! Door!" he shouted but remembered that Guy wasn't home. Salamanders, two of them, down by the train station. And just after an all-nighter dealing with some drakes. When it rained it poured. Well, Guy was probably hoping for some rain. Salamanders weren't fans of water.

He gave his axe one final wipe down and made his way to the door. He opened it without asking who it was. If it was any kinda danger, he had his hand on his pistol.

"Cindy?"

"Brett, long time…"

Brett turned and let Cindy close the door herself. He returned to his weapon cleaning. Cindy winced at some of the apparatus on the table. The meat-hooks, especially. Silver tipped. Like everything else.

"An expensive collection."

"A necessary collection," Brett replied. "And it gets a lot of use."

"I see that…"

She rounded the table to face Brett, and sat down on a chair, without permission.

Brett ignored her as he scrubbed at the mechanism of his one pistol. He had held it too close to a vamp's head and there was blood and guts encrusted in it.

"Brett…" Cindy started, and Brett couldn't help but feel anger rise at the tone in her voice. Pitying. Disgustingly so. Why did he need pity? He didn't need pity! He needed help. Help finding Kat.

"Guy and I have been killing vampires," Brett said, cutting her off. "They all say they have no connection to Blood Cartel. That Blood Cartel is dead. That leaves Sanguineas."

"Brett…I don't think this is helping…"

"Then what will?!" Brett shouted, bending the shaft of the plastic toothbrush he was using to scrub away at the pistol.

"Don't shout at me," Cindy said, straightening her back. "We are all looking for Kat."

"Like the demon hunter? I'm surprised he can even walk. He's ancient. And fat help he's been. If he had been watching her back like he was supposed to, she would still be with us."

"Conrad and I are looking into things. Actually, looking into things. We aren't torturing innocent vamp…"

"Innocent? Don't even fucking think that, Cindy! Those monsters…"

Brett couldn't finish the sentence. He shook his head and focused on his cleaning.

"They have her, Cindy. I just know it," Brett muttered, almost helplessly. "I just need to kill a few more. Capture a few more. Then I'll find where they have her."

"If the vampires really have her, Brett, you know what it probably means if she's still alive?"

Brett froze, and looked Cindy in the eyes. She looked stern. Robotic. But there was a hint of fear in her eyes.

"But I don't think they have her," Cindy continued. "There're other leads. Secret societies, necromancers. The fucking Necrolord that you guys were hunting. If it was vampires, she'd have been found already."

Or turned, Brett thought, and wanted to vomit.

Brett started reassembling his pistol.

"Sun's going down. I need to go hunting."

"You need to go hunting," Cindy said. "But this isn't about Kat, is it?"

He winced.

"There are more monsters in the world than vampires, Brett. Don't let your hate of them blind you to that. If you really like Kat as much as I do, then you will keep an open mind. You'll start looking in more places. Help Conrad and me. We'll find her if there is anything left to find."

"They have her," Brett murmured, standing up and packing up his weapons. "And she's alive. She can't be dead. She's Kat."

Cindy didn't reply as Brett started putting on his equipment. She walked towards the door and looked back at him one last time, shaking her head.

Brett heard the door shut behind her. He only stared at the Mauser pistol on the bookshelf, reminding himself of why he was doing this.

"I'll save her. I have to."

Chapter 7. Talking to the Dead

Treth didn't overtly tell me to kill Candace since we were let out of the cell. I felt an internal conflict within my spirit companion and felt the same discordance within my own mind. We didn't talk of slaying our necromancer host, even if we both thought about it. But if I had struggled to kill Jeremiah Cox, and still felt the regretful vibrations of recoil as I pulled the trigger on Cornelius Black, how could I kill a little girl?

Easily, my hunter voice told me. *Knives in the kitchen. Slit her throat. Smash her head into the countertop. Strangle her. Smother her. Take the wire from any of the contraptions around the stronghold and garrotte her. Kill her like she killed the countless innocent people with her army of undead.*

But it wasn't that easy. And I felt Treth was coming to the same realisation. A child, no matter how evil, was not meant to die. And I wasn't even sure that Candace was evil. Sure, I knew what she had done. And I heard the derangement in her voice sometimes. But I also saw a young girl who had lost her parents. I saw me.

Candace explained to me that I couldn't leave the compound for my own protection. I didn't argue, lest I offend her and risk seeing how evil she could truly be, but she gave me a justification anyway.

Not only was that she-vamp, Charlene Terhoff, still after me, so was the Conclave. Candace believed that the Conclave now saw me as a rogue asset. Or at least an exhausted one. And if Drake was what they did to assets that were past their expiration date, then perhaps I was safer behind these walls. I just hoped they didn't take out their ire on my friends. If they did, then they would have true hell to pay.

Candace excused herself after our chat, promising to retrieve some ramen. I saw a hint of pride in her eye as she made the promise. She was proud of her ability to go grocery shopping. Proud! But if I recalled how she made her money, and who her agents were on the outside, I saw nothing to be proud of.

Strangely, I felt a sense of loss as Candace left the room. I couldn't put my finger on it but, without another soul nearby, I felt an eerie loneliness that I seldom ever felt. And at this time, with what had happened...I didn't want to be alone with my thoughts.

"Let's look around," I said to Treth, more to prompt him to speak. To fill the silence in the room.

Treth grunted his assent. I wished he'd say something. Anything. I needed noise.

I made my way first to the bookshelf. While the small shelf in my cell was a motley collection of arbitrary literature and not-so-literature, this shelf was much more erudite. One shelf was devoted to philosophy, metaphysics, ethics. Stuff that I seldom read and would much less have expected a 14-year-old to read. On another shelf was a collection of classics. Tolstoy, Homer, Aesop, Dickens, Wu Cheng'en…A disparate assortment of the types of books that defined cultures, and that everyone lied about reading. The last segment of shelving was filled with textbooks. School textbooks. From primary to high school level, and some higher. One was a first-year university general course for weyline usage. Idly, I withdrew the book from the shelf and heard papers rustle. As I pulled out the textbook, a brightly coloured, illustrated cover was revealed. I reached through the space I had made and took out what seemed to be a comic. A superhero comic. It looked well-read, but still maintained in relatively good condition. It had been enjoyed, not abused. Behind other textbooks, I found more comics. Some superhero, some westerns, some sci-fi. In general, the advised age for each comic was around 16-years and younger.

"Peculiar," I commented, paging through a graphic novelisation of Warpwars, the violence toned down for a younger audience.

"Evil may wear a white mask, but it bears a heart of black," Treth recounted, quoting someone.

"Who said that? Your master?"

"Gorgo," he said, simply.

"The poltergeist?"

"She wasn't always a poltergeist."

"Ah, yeah. Sorry."

I continued looking at the pictures in the comic, even as I felt Treth's mind wander to dark places.

"Treth?" I asked. He may be silent now, but I needed the distraction.

"I'm fine. Just remembering stuff. Not a big deal."

"Remembering, for us, is always a big deal."

He paused, and then chuckled, without any humour.

"That's about right." He sighed, heavily. But I felt no weight lift from his soul.

"What…who was Gorgo to you?" I asked, partly to make conversation and partly to fill the void. But as I asked the question, I regretted it. Not only because I did not want to bring up bad memories for Treth, but also because I feared his answer.

"She was…my friend," he answered, and I felt a sense of relief. Why did I feel relief? But I felt another emotion wash off Treth to me. A deep anguish, awfully familiar. I thought of Colin, and my breath caught in my throat. I closed the comic and leant up against the bookshelf, looking at the floor.

"You watched her die," I said. It wasn't a question. I knew he had. As if through Colin's death, I saw Gorgo's.

Treth was shocked but assented.

"My brother," he said. He didn't have to say any more.

"Let's see what else we can find in this place," I said.

Treth and I both were glad to have that conversation over as I back-tracked my way to my cell. Candace had gone through the opposite door, and I didn't feel like running into whatever she was doing. I also didn't feel like running into that creature – Petunia – or any of the flesh-puppets, but did I really have a choice? I needed to get the lay of the land. If walking past undead beasts was a requirement for that, then so be it.

Even though I feared walking past the undead and their uncaring gazes, all the flesh-puppets had disappeared from the hall. Candace must have sent them away. There were closed cell doors like mine lining the rim of the curving passage. I didn't look into them for fear of what they contained, but I felt that Candace must have housed her flesh-puppets. Was it because I was visibly uncomfortable around them? Did she care?

"That creature in the darkness…" Treth said.

"Petunia," I offered.

"The creature," he continued. "It can't really be alive. It has to be undead. Or some sort of blood-shaped mutant."

"We aren't necromancers, thank Athena," I replied, glancing up the hallway and sideways at the closed cell doors. My hands felt cold without steel and my outer thighs were uncomfortably light without sheaths. "We don't know nearly enough of what they are capable of. I agree with you, it is hard to fathom, but what if she is right? What if the creature is actually alive?"

"Then we must expand our hate to more than just the dead."

I frowned, but I couldn't help but agree as I imagined faint giggling in the distance.

I crossed past my cell, door open and the contents undisturbed, and continued down the hall. It was a mirror of the other side, curving again, suggesting that this hallway was a crescent, and the structure itself was round.

"Round structure. Reason?" Treth asked, as if testing me. It had been a while since he had taken the role of mentor. I had kinda missed it. We had both been so lost lately that neither of us was really teaching the other. We had both been drowning when trying to learn to swim.

"The circle is ritualistic," I answered. "Most wizardry requires a circle and circle structures can help feed the local weyline into a central ritual site."

"That, and also its defensive nature. A circle means an unclear angle of attack. Unlike a square, a circle is an unbroken layer of defence. It provides easy routes of traffic for defenders, while providing layers and layers of confusing, winding hallways to its attackers."

"Fight any sieges in Avathor?"

"No. Well, yes. But not against any castles. We defended castles. Some stood for a while against the undead, but as supplies ran out, the undead attacked us from behind, the necromancers reanimating fallen peasants from within the fortifications. We moved our war effort to sparsely populated hermitages and monasteries. And eventually, those fell too…"

Treth trailed off and I felt him begin to brood.

Well done, Kat! Be a downer for everyone.

I thought of Colin, unbidden, and bit my lip. I changed my thoughts to Andy and his twisting form and flesh, sprouting fur and claw. I clenched my fists. I'd kill him, and I'd make sure he suffered a hundred times worse than Colin.

But my anger abated, and my pace slowed.

Killing Andy wasn't going to bring him back.

I still didn't cry as I came to a door in what I decided to call the west wing, despite having no accurate compass. My cell-phone had no signal, no internet connection, and the compass app (which was never accurate) just kept spinning in circles. So, when without any form of verifiable knowledge, one can be excused for making things up just a bit.

I opened the plain wooden door to reveal a warmly lit lounge area, adorned with a red rug, two dark leather armchairs, and more shelves, with hundreds more books. As I moved further into the room, I saw a dining area, dominated by a long oak table, with four chairs spaced far apart the long table top. At the head of the table was a bowl of soggy, half-eaten cereal. Multicoloured. Sweet stuff. Candace had spilled some sugar onto the table. She hadn't cleaned it up. I couldn't help but smile a bit but stopped myself.

Yes, she was a messy teenager like I was...am...but she was still a necromancer.

I surveyed the bookshelves and found that not all of them were books. There was a record-player on a low-shelf, and a pile of records next to it. Only one album cover wasn't covered in dust. A black and white picture of a man and woman. The man's foot on a stool, holding the hand of a woman wearing a black, semi-translucent cape. The name of the album was *Rumours,* by *Fleetwood Mac.*

I turned on the record-player, carefully as I tried to work with this archaic technology I only saw in movies. I placed the arm of the player onto the record and heard the unmistakable drum beat and guitar twangs that introduced *The Chain.*

I smiled and began mouthing the lyrics. My eyes moistened as the song continued, and I blinked. I felt Treth watching me. Curious.

"My parents liked this song," I said. He nodded. He understood.

I stood still, waiting for the song to end. As it ended and transitioned to *You Make Loving Fun*, I exited the warm room and entered the hallway opposite the one I had just come from. It seemed identical, curving to form a crescent. Distantly, I heard what sounded like bubbles, steam-hissing and birds tweeting.

With *Fleetwood Mac* behind me, I advanced down the hall. Christine McVie's voice became quieter and quieter as I proceeded further into the darkness, finally coming to a double-door crafted of aluminium and steel-plating.

I opened the door, half-expecting more books, more records, and more childish things to suggest that Candace was not a monster. I found confirmation not of her humanity, however, but that she was the Necrolord. Shelves of jarred organs. Human eyes pinned to cork-wall. A human hand, twisting a screwdriver impotently into the air. A crow, spitted on a spike with a cork on the end, let out a squawk. It had one eye and was flapping its rotting wings as it remained stationary on a smooth, metal lab-table.

I held on to the doorframe to steady myself.

"See, Kat?" Treth asked, vindicated. "She isn't just a child."

My pale complexion and oncoming nausea must have made him less satisfied with our discovery.

"Kat," he said again, much more tenderly. "Necromancy is dark magic. And I've seen what it does to people. We saw what she's done already. This can't be a surprise to you."

"She's…" I almost gagged as I saw a ripe human corpse, its insides opened up like a frog in a biology lab. Buckets of sharp bone shards lay to the side, with a pair of bloodied rubber gloves discarded atop them. I felt a stinging sensation in my back. I had pock-marked scars where bone shrapnel had been extracted by healers. It still hurt sometimes. I had been in the hospital for a long time after that. Too long, watching Colin suffer as he saw me suffer.

"She's just a child," I said, finally.

"She has started evil early," Treth said. "All the worse for her. The darkness will be truly entrenched by the time she reaches the age of most necromancers."

"Can't…can't we save her?"

"I thought I could save my brother," Treth said. He didn't finish. We both knew how that story ended.

I looked up as I heard a faint voice speaking in the distance. Pushing down my revulsion about the contents of what I could only loosely call a laboratory, I walked softly towards the sound, through a door leading further within the circle. Immediately, I was faced with a waft of cold air. The kind of air you find in the entry-way before a freezer. I shivered, and not from the cold. A freezer was essential for a necromancer. Needed to keep corpses fresh. Rotting zombies were scary and disgusting, but they didn't make efficient fighters.

I didn't know what drew me further into the freezer, and closer to the voice, other than dangerous curiosity. I could have just ignored the voices. I could have returned to the record-player and the lit fire. But I needed to know more. I needed to understand my necromancer host and find out if she was a monster or a human.

I stopped outside of an open metal freezer door and listened to Candace speak to someone who did not reply.

"She seems nice," Candace said. "Didn't try to stab me."

"Swords? No, no. But there's knives all around. She could do it any time. But she didn't. I think that makes us friends."

She sounded happy, but in that carefree tone was a hint of sadness.

"I hope she will be my friend," Candace said, sounding properly sad now. "Not just because of what happened to her, or me, or us, or them...I don't know. But, it hurts. I can't even cry anymore. But the voices don't come as often when she's around. And it only hurts when it should. When I'm hating it. But I can't make it hurt all the time. I have to let it in a little. A little bit. But not for a lot longer."

I considered peeking, to see who she was talking to, but thought better of it.

"Do...you...will you forgive me, dad?" she said, softly. No reply, obviously. She laughed, sadly.

"I ask that every single time, don't I? But I hope you do. For everything. And if you forgive me...maybe then I will realise what I've done is wrong. But by then, it won't have been. It will be worth it. Just to see you again."

Before Candace could find me eavesdropping, I snuck out of the hallway and back towards my room/cell. Along the way, I didn't speak to Treth. I only thought of my parents and of Colin.

If I could only see them again. And I felt a little voice inside my head tell me that I could.

Chapter 8. Growing Up

The blood was made black as it nestled into the barely settled dark concrete flooring. Only a distant streetlight, obscured by the storm, shone. The light formed patterns in the dampness, a shard of light in the puddle of blood on the floor, and a glint off the metal caked in red, being held in my hand. I felt snot, sweat and tears cling to my face, mingling with the rain. My hair clung to my forehead, even as the rest of it was hidden underneath a black hoodie. Rain drenched my clothing and mixed with the blood staining my cuffs and front. The water didn't clean the red away. It only diluted it. Spread it. What I did never really went away. It just faded and faded. Until it mattered less and less. But it was still there. It'd always be there.

Even under cover, I heard the storm bellow outside, rain pelting the roof of this abandoned building, forever under construction. Gusts of sharp rain shot through the open window-holes, like volleys of bullets.

And a man I'd only just met lay bloodied on the ground, his chest pockmarked with reddening holes. His shirt had been white before. It was dark now and the parts of it illuminated by the distant streetlight showed red.

I had never feared the now dead man. A part of me knew that I should have. Years before, I would have run away from the man who asked a 12-year-old girl to follow him into a construction site, in the dead of night. But I wasn't that little girl any more. And while the man thought himself the predator, he did not see the knife I held behind my back. And when he saw the desperation, hesitation and fear of something very much different from him, in my eyes, it was too late.

It wasn't like stabbing into a steak. Cooked meat has a different texture. It is drier. Artificial, even. It isn't like real meat. Naturally warm. Still flowing. Wet. Really wet. And no steak I've ever eaten has squelched the way my knife did in the man's chest. Again. And again. He cried out, but thunder hammered, and rain pelted. Nobody would hear him. Ironic, isn't it? He wanted to use the sound of the weather to ensure nobody heard me. The Mentor was clear about that. He was a bad man. An evil man. The type of man who preys on desperate little girls. I shouldn't feel anything for killing him. Yet, as he cried out and I felt the sick resistance of his skin and flesh against my blade, I wanted to scream. I wanted to pull back and run. All I could do is let the tears fall from my eyes, as I pulled the knife, pushed it forward, pulled it back. Over and over.

Until he stopped moving, and the distant streetlight was all that showed what I had done.

I stared at the corpse for a few minutes before the Mentor arrived, the scuffing of his sneakers on the concrete floor was only audible when he was a few metres behind me. I didn't turn. I knew it could only be him. He had promised it would only be him.

"Are you okay?" he asked, his voice filled with warmth and concern. "Did he hurt you?"

No, I wanted to say. *But I hurt me. I'm hurting. And my head hurts. And my joints hurt. And the words are hurting again. And my hand hurts from gripping the knife handle. I want to go home.*

Instead, I said. "No, Mentor. He is dead."

"Good...good," he said, slowly. He approached me, closer, and I felt his piercing gaze look at me from the side. I didn't look at him. My eyes were glued to the bloodied man, splayed on the ground.

"You are crying?" the Mentor asked, but it sounded like an accusation.

My breath caught in my throat. Not at fear of scolding. The Mentor never scolded me. No, I was afraid that I had failed him. That I had done something wrong. That I had let down the Mentor. And if I had failed the Mentor, would I be able to master this magic? Would I be able to bring back my parents?

"No..." I began but stopped as he rubbed his finger below my eyes, wiping away tears.

"He deserved to die."

"I know," I said.

"It will become easier, in time," the Mentor said, his voice filled with warmth and sincerity. It calmed me. It always did. I was never afraid of the Mentor. He would never hurt me. I was only afraid that I would let him down. And for all he had done for me, I could not fail him. But his wiping away my tears stopped more from falling, and I felt my breathing calm. I took a deep breath, taking in the earthy smell of rain and the hint of iron from the blood.

"I hope you understand why you had to be the one to do this," the Mentor said, a hint of concern in his voice.

"Yes, Mentor. The raised should have their blood spilt by their benefactor."

Benefactor. Necromancer. The Graffscripp used both interchangeably.

"Correct, for some raised. But not this one."

"Mentor?" I asked, my voice cracking just a bit. Did I just kill this man unnecessarily? When there were truckloads of corpses in Mentor's freezer.

"You will not always have freezers or graveyards, my precious student. It is our lot that sometimes we may find ourselves in a deathless space but surrounded by enemies. Our ability to defend ourselves should not be limited by the death we surround ourselves with. Do you understand?"

I didn't reply immediately as I stared at the man, trying to picture what he had planned to do with me after I offered myself to him for a few dollars. It didn't help. I had not been afraid. The Mentor had told me I would be okay. And he had never lied to me. But then he wasn't lying now.

"I understand, Mentor."

"Good."

I felt his warm smile, lighting up the darkness and the cold of the unfinished room. At that moment, I knew what

I had known for the past few years. I could trust the Mentor completely.

"I'm ready, Master."

I only called him master when were about to do a ritual. I felt it helped me concentrate. I owed my knowledge to him. Reverence helped me remember that. It helped the words flow better.

"Do you remember the words?"

I hesitated, as the words in the back of my head flared up and threatened to sear into my skull. I nodded.

"Concentrate on them, Candace," he said, firmly. "And channel your will into the man before you. Forget what he was. Forget what he did. Forget what you did to him. He is only meat. Only flesh and bone. But through you, he gains new purpose. New life."

"Master, how will I control him? The zombies, they still won't listen to me…"

I had created many since Igor had died, but none had listened. They only went on rampages, searching for flesh. The Mentor never scolded me, but he must have been disappointed. What type of necromancer couldn't control a zombie?

"You aren't creating anything so brutish or bestial as the famished dead, Candace. You're extending your will. Creating new limbs. You are not making a servant now. You are spreading yourself through bodies that no longer have souls that need them."

"Is that what a flesh puppet is?"

"Yes. And you will need not worry about it turning on you or me. It is an extension of your very being. A total and unflagging…"

The Mentor was interrupted by police sirens. In the distance.

"They aren't coming for us," he said, calmly. "But we should do this quickly nonetheless. Begin channelling. Do you feel the weyline?"

I closed my eyes and sent out my better senses, feeling for the weyline that channelled through this area, leading to the Vortex. I sent out invisible tendrils of perception, grasping in the darkness, until I felt it. It smelt like incense, burning. Acrid, yet somehow sweet. I reached towards it, and it recoiled. Dark weylines were always harder to tame. The Mentor said they had their own will. They would not be wasted on pettier forms of magic. They demanded a worthy cause.

I sent forth my will to communicate with the darkness.

"I come to raise the dead," I said, wordlessly, towards the dark.

It stopped but didn't approach. I had done this plenty of times. The Mentor said I was good at it.

"The light is not here to smother you," I said. "I accept you, so that you accept me."

I felt a sting as the dark weyline rushed towards me. My breath caught in my throat, as it often did when I absorbed so much dark power.

"Incant the words," the Mentor said, quietly yet firmly.

I began. The first words flowed easily, but as I got to the middle, I stammered, and halted. I snivelled, even as I felt the darkness and the Mentor's gaze.

"It's okay, Candace," Mentor spoke tenderly. "It hurts now, but it won't after you're done."

I muscled through the next few words but felt sharp stabs in my gut as I mispronounced a few words. Stuttered over others. Missed a syllable.

I was failing. I was failing the Mentor. And the darkness knew it. It wouldn't accept me. Perhaps that is why the zombies disobeyed me? Because I struggled to speak simple words. Because I wasn't powerful enough for it.

The corpse didn't move. Tears fell from my eyes, and some sobs choked my incantation.

"Start again," the Mentor said, and I began again, the pain in my head increasing three-fold the second-time. I stopped and clutched my head.

"Keep going, Candace," he said.

I did, even as my head felt that it had split open, and that my brain was slowly pouring out. I kept uttering every toxic word, letting them spill onto the concrete like vomit.

"You can do it," Mentor said and, while he sounded kind, I could sense his impatience.

I tried to speak faster. To not fail the master, but my words became more and more garbled, until I didn't understand nor recognise what I was saying.

The Mentor kept trying to encourage me. Kept whispering words of wisdom and kindness, even as I sputtered vomit onto the ground before me and wept openly. Until he stopped, and I kept going. And finally, I could not go on any longer. I stopped and fell to my knees.

The Mentor approached me, as I cried, tears falling onto my jeans, and vomit-specked spittle coating my lips. He put his hand on my shoulder.

"I guess you don't really want to see your parents again," he said, simply, but I felt it as if it was a sword through the heart. Slowly, I got back up to my feet, and he released my shoulder.

I began the words, and the pain returned a hundred-fold. And I said another, and it returned more painful than anything I could imagine. I worked through the words. Slowly. Steadily. And I wanted to die. But the corpse twitched, and I felt the pain abate. I sped up, the words becoming clearer. And as each limb twitched, it became easier and easier, until finally, I released the final word as a crescendo. The corpse, my new flesh puppet, rose as I willed it to do so. I sent a command to it. To kneel. To show reverence. Not to me. To the Mentor.

It knelt. And I felt the Mentor's hand on my shoulder. Not scolding. Not accusatory. But acknowledging me. I was no longer crying. I was laughing.

Chapter 9. Leads

Brett thrust his silver stake forward with what he'd like to think was blinding speed. Unfortunately, what is fast for a human, is often very slow for a vampire. The vamp side-stepped the stab and karate chopped Brett's arm. With a wince of pain, he dropped the stake. Close combat fighting was a lot harder than he remembered. Yet, Kat made it look so easy.

The vamp hissed, sending spittle to land on Brett's exposed forehead. He was thankful that he had remembered to wear at least half a mask. If he was operating during the day, he would have needed a lot more. Vamp hunting – at least this type of vamp hunting – was illegal after all. But Brett wasn't one to obey unjust laws. Monsters didn't stop being monsters just because a piece of magical paper deemed it so. And Brett wouldn't let them have impunity because they had suckered people into thinking they were just humans with an allergy to the sun and special dietary requirements. And Brett, especially, wouldn't let them get away with holding Kat hostage. And even if it took every blood-sucker in the city, he would find where she was being held.

Brett jumped back, drawing his silver-trim bowie knife. His ankle ached as it impacted on the ground. Old wounds. He splayed his arms, holding the knife pointed towards the vampire, metres away. A road-flare and the moon lit up the room. Vamps didn't need light. Brett did. And he didn't trust electrical lighting in a vampire lair. Flares lasted long enough, and vampires hated them.

"I can do this till the sun comes up," Brett said, feinting an advance.

The vampire hissed, backing into the far corner. It bared its fangs. Longer than normal for a vamp. About as long as a forefinger. Must be extendable. That was rare. Brett had killed many vampires before. Only five had retractable and extendable fangs. It wasn't a useful mutation. The human mouth, even with fangs, was not a potent weapon. Only bestial vampires, who preyed on livestock, tended to utilise the fangs well. For a hunter of humans, they were basically just for show.

"Where is Terhoff?"

The vamp hissed again. Like a very angry snake or cat. It bit down, making a sickening chomping sound. In its current state, it was more animal than anything resembling a human. Brett knew that vampires were beasts. All of them, at their core. But some were just better at hiding the animal inside.

Brett and the vampire maintained eye-contact. Usually, he wouldn't risk looking a vamp in the eye, but this one was too far gone to use any charms. It was full predator now, and predators had certain common traits. Maintaining eye-sight was about dominance. If Brett dropped his gaze, the vamp would go in for the kill. By staring into the sickly red eyes of this bloodsucker, Brett was issuing a challenge, and, in the primal laws of beasts, he said.

"Come here if you want to die."

The vampire moved slowly, sidling along, the wall at its back. The flare flickered. Brett kept the monster's gaze, moving to face him. Hand on his knife. Breathing slowed. He heard nothing but the beating of his own heart, and the wheezing of the vampire.

The flare flickered out and the moon only showed a black blur before Brett was knocked onto the floor. He felt his knife dig into flesh. He pulled it out and stabbed again. Something dug into his hand. He grunted as it broke skin, scraping and lacerating his hand as he pushed away the vamp's head. He felt a sickly wet tongue lap up the blood on his hand. Panic threatened to take over and Brett stabbed more furiously, looking for a vital spot in the dark. A fist hit his gut and he let go of the knife hilt. He grabbed onto the vampire's side and felt cold flesh.

Had he underestimated the creature? Fledgling vampires still had body warmth. It took more than one or two mutations to start losing blood circulation.

Brett lifted his free arm but couldn't find the blade. He instead moved his hand to the vampire's head, holding its chin and attempting to wrest it away from his hand. The vamp held his hand in a death-grip, lapping up all the blood it could get. Brett tried to kick it off, but he was only a human. Against a monster. The vampire stopped, suddenly, as Brett still kicked and punched at it, and Brett could see its hungry eyes glow in the dark. It went for the throat.

A deafening ratta-tat-tat brought the vampire's head up. Or was it the bullets drilling through its brain? The vampire spasmed as rounds pierced its skull and chest. It fell backwards with a whine and a splutter. Another flare was thrown in, landing just by the wounded vampire's head. It recoiled, but the silver tipped lead in its cranium prevented it from doing much else.

"Stick to guns," Guy said, tossing Brett a small bandage, which he promptly wrapped around his wounded hand. The vamp had sealed a lot of the wound with its saliva already, but there was still some bleeding.

Guy walked up to the vampire, twisted on the floor. He tapped his fingers on the side of his machine-pistols, thinking, and then fired two more rounds into the vamp's head. It stopped moving.

"Might…" Brett stopped speaking, still out of breath. Guy waited patiently for him to get his bearings. When Brett's breathing was back to normal, Guy offered him a hand up.

"Might as well behead it. It's gone feral."

Guy shrugged. "Yes, boss."

He withdrew a forward-curving blade called a kukri, held the vampire by its hair, and with one swipe, took off its head. He discarded the head by the rest of the body. The sun would shine through the window in the morning and all evidence would become ash. It was very easy to get away with killing vampires. Even if they survived, their bodies absorbed DNA evidence. And if they died in the sun, then ash didn't carry any evidence either. And don't worry about the silver rounds. Silver was too soft to leave anything a forensics team would need. It burst on impact. Trying to trace a silver round back to its firer was like trying to find which beach some pocket sand came from. And that assumes that the forensics team would care. Cops were a lot of things, but most of them shared Brett and Guy's disdain for vampires. Cops were the ones who were called out when some vamp punk thought their powers were justification enough to not take no for an answer from a girl at the club. Police in Hope City were many negative things, but they were savvy when it came to blood-suckers. Made Brett and Guy's job easier.

"How'd the others go?" Brett asked, examining his hand. It didn't hurt anymore. Vamp saliva was a form of anaesthetic. Helped them feed on sleeping victims.

"First one was a clawer. Had to plant him quick. Got nothing."

Guy holstered his pistol and raised two fingers.

"Second one almost got away, but he was a flyer. Wings weren't fully developed yet, so he fell to the ground. Legs won't heal before the morning, but I put a few rounds in him any way."

"Fuck. Did you manage to get any information?"

"Third. Dead."

"Fuck," Brett repeated.

"But, did tell me something from beyond the grave."

Guy tossed a small object that Brett deftly caught and held up to the moonlight.

"For Qamata's sake, use a damn flashlight. We're killing the things, not trying to be like them."

"Flashlight isn't any good in a melee," Brett replied, but took a small one out of his vest pocket.

"Why do you insist on fighting them hand to hand?"

Brett ignored him and examined the object. It was a pocket knife. Small thing. No use in a fight. Utility. He opened it up. The edge was silver.

"Third vamp had that on him."

"Vamp infighting?" Brett offered. "In case he needed to put a scratch on a room-mate?"

"I doubt it. He'd probably invest in something a bit bigger then. In a fight, that'd probably just tickle. I think it's something else."

Guy withdrew a cell-phone from his vest pocket. Blood was smeared over the corner. A text message was open.

"Alley between 15 and 17 Farthing Rd. Morningsville. 500ml. Don't skimp this time," Brett read. "This what I think it is?"

"Blood trade," Guy said, affirming Brett's suspicions.

Brett glowered in the darkness. Guy was impassive, but Brett knew that his friend was just as disgusted. It was the reason that Guy hadn't gone back to his hometown. Zulu occupation hadn't been that oppressive for over a decade, but there was nothing really to go back to. Everyone Guy grew up with was hooked on vamp-blood. They worked themselves to the bone for vampire bosses, just for a drop. And Guy couldn't do anything about it. Hope City might let the bloodsuckers live, but the Empire elevated them to nobility status. If he took the head off one vamp, and somehow got away with it, there were hundreds more to follow. So, Guy came to Hope City and never looked back. He'd even stopped sending his pay check to the Transkei resistance every month. There was no more resistance.

"We're gonna crash this dealer?" Brett asked.

"Of course, we fucki…" Guy snapped, but stopped himself. He breathed slowly. He liked to be calm. Collected. Brett preferred hot rage. "You want to find your girl, don't you? Let's go."

They exited the room and re-entered the dingy apartment hallway. No self-respecting human could live in a place like this, but Brett and Guy knew all too well that most of Hope City did live in these sorts of conditions. And worse. And whenever a developer managed to get Council approval to do something about it, necromancer warlords, gangsters and vampire cartels chased them out. Hope City didn't need to be a sea of slums around the jewel of the South, but its monsters and people ensured that it stayed that way. Over 16 million people, with the bulk living in dark weylines, surrounded by monsters.

Brett wondered everyday how the city still survived.

"She's not my girl," Brett replied, long after the statement.

"Then why are we doing this? Every night. Skipping out on proper bounties. Doing the bare minimum to keep our licenses. Risking arrest."

"Cops won't investigate some ash-piles. Vampire lobby can't get them to do anything when the cops know they'll get paid if they're sitting or standing. For once, the public sector works."

"Then risking vampires. We signed up to Drakenbane for a reason. We were over vampires. For years. And then Kat dragged us along to save her goth friend."

"You saying you didn't want to save her?"

"I'm saying that we made a promise to each other. And ourselves. No more vampires. Not because the bastards don't need to die, but because it isn't good for us."

Guy stopped and indicated Brett's face.

"When last did you sleep?"

"Earlier today."

"Naps don't count. And you know who else sleeps during the day? Vampires!"

"Vampires don't sleep."

"You know what I meant!"

Guy put up his hands, exasperated. They exited the apartment building onto a dead street. No lights. No cars except their black van. Poor neighbourhood. It had to be when even the vampires were living in squalor.

Brett reached to open the van door, but Guy stopped him, placing his hand on Brett's shoulder.

"Brett...you know that I'm behind you every step of the way. But I need to know why you're doing this. And not just to save a girl. Any girl. Cause there's a thousand girls being taken by vampires every night. Why this girl, and not any of the others?"

Brett clenched his fist over the door handle, but sighed, loosening his hand and letting it fall limply to his side.

"I don't know, Guy. It's just...ugh...it was much simpler when I was just calling her Katty and pissing her off. Was so much fun. She'd make this face, like she wanted to skewer me with those swords of hers."

Brett grinned, but then frowned. "But even though I pissed her off, she still trusted me...to help her find her friend. How could I say no? What should I have said? That vampires make me into a monster? That I enjoy killing them and that I hate myself for that? That I was programmed to hate them above everything else. How could I tell her that her friend's gotta die because I'm trying to get over being a child soldier in a fucking death squad?"

Brett was shouting, and he realised it. He stopped.

"You love her?" Guy asked.

Brett looked away, feeling a stab of shock in his heart.

"No, no. She's a friend. A close friend...." He started blabbering out excuses. Guy cut him off with a laugh.

"You always liked the crazy ones."

"Crazy?" Brett exclaimed, aghast. "Kat isn't crazy. She understands what needs to be done better than most of this fucking city. Sees the darkness and doesn't hide it behind some fucking shiny towers. She's saner than almost anyone at the agency. Probably more competent, as well."

"You haven't seen it?" Guy said, raising his eyebrow, quizzically. He moved to the other side of the van. Brett and Guy entered. Guy continued after they pulled off and began the drive.

"She talks to herself. When she thinks nobody is looking."

"Plenty of people talk to themselves. It's because they lack intelligent company."

"It's not just that. She also stops to listen. Looks up and bites her lip. As if someone is replying."

"If she's so crazy, you don't have to help me find her."

Brett winced as it came out sounding a bit too petulant. Guy laughed.

"Come on, Brett. I like the chick. As you said, she's one of the best hunters this city has to offer. But even if I didn't like her, I must admit that I've missed killing vamps."

Brett looked at his friend, in the driver's seat. He looked, in a way, happy.

"What are we?" Brett asked, not knowing why he asked, or the answer.

"Crazy, probably." Guy grinned. "And that's how I know these things. Takes one to know one."

***

The dealer was also a vampire. But one of the more human-looking variety. Had short fangs in a mouth of charming, pearly-white teeth. With his blonde hair and baby face, he must've tricked a lot of housewives into thinking he was harmless. Brett enjoyed shoving a meat-hook through his cheek and using it to drag him further into the alley, where nobody could hear him.

"Smash them," Brett ordered.

"Yes, boss," Guy answered sarcastically, pulling a tray of vials out of a cooler bag and tossing them on the ground. The dealer winced and struggled with every volley of vials that Guy threw on the ground. Glass and vamp blood fell into the crevices of the badly set concrete. Brett didn't care if some rats drank it. A rat addicted to vampire blood could cause some problems for them. Nothing like a group of rats tailing a vampire in the dark. May even chase a fledgling into the sunlight.

A scruffy looking student, wearing a beanie with the word *Maties* on it, came further into the alley. Looked like the junkie type. Guy and Brett just stared daggers at him and he turned back and hoofed it. He wasn't far gone enough with the addiction to take on two muscle-bound, black-clad guys covered in guns and blades.

All the vials smashed, Guy ripped through the bag with a knife and threw the shredded remains onto the ground.

Brett removed the hook, but still held his bowie to the dealer's throat. The vampire sputtered, but even then, the flesh in his cheeks was knitting back together. Wouldn't even leave a scar.

The dealer-vamp got his breath back and then stared daggers at Brett.

"What the fuck, dudes? That was some prime shit you just wasted. What type of fucking racket you running, bro?"

"Cut the shit, leach," Brett said. "Where's Terhoff?"

"Terhoff? Don't know who the fuck that is. If this is about my dues, I told DV to let Kruger know I'll double up next week. But now I can't even do fucking that. So, you can go…"

"Kruger?" Brett asked, interrupting him. The edge of his blade bit further into his neck.

"Ow! Fucking silver, dude? That's not playing fair."

"What did you mean Kruger?" Brett yelled.

"You fucking fledglings, bro? The Kruger. Violetta Kruger. Of San-fucking-guineas."

Brett and Guy couldn't reply. Brett felt his empty hand shiver, but he held his knife steady.

Kruger. Violetta Kruger of the Sanguineas Cartel…was back in Hope City.

"Where's she staying?"

"That fuck-off huge mansion in Constantia. Why you asking me? She sent you, didn't she?"

The dealer's expression changed slowly, first to confusion, and then utter dismay as he realised what he had done.

"Fuck!" he cried out and tried to dart away. Big mistake. Brett's bowie bit in so hard that it almost beheaded him. Stopped right by the windpipe. He passed out.

Brett let him fall to the ground. No blood spilt from his eviscerated neck. Vamps didn't bleed like humans did. They got a trickle where they got cut, but no gushes of blood. Couldn't bleed them out. They didn't even need their own blood, technically. Just made them hungrier when they're out of it.

"She's back," Guy said, simply.

"She was bound to come back eventually."

"I thought that the Magocracy would set her straight."

"No more Corps to stop vampires there," Brett replied, sourly. "And I don't think even the Corps could deal with her. If they even knew she was a vampire."

"I heard she's old. That means she should have noticeable mutations."

"She's Earthborn, so not too old. But way older than she looks."

Brett indicated for Guy to help him lift up the unconscious dealer. They could still interrogate him for more info.

"Only mutations she has is pale skin and fangs. Nothing else noticeable," Brett continued. "But here's the thing…nobody survives a fight with her to report back on her mutations."

"That's because nobody fights her," Guy retorted.

"And that. I suspect she has some charm mutations."

"That means eye-protection. Got it."

Brett stopped and looked at his friend.

"We really doing this? Going after Violetta Kruger?"

"Who else is gonna help you get your girl back?" Guy grinned, but it looked forced. He frowned. "And besides, these last weeks have reminded me of why I became a hunter in the first place. I might not be able to cut the head off the snake back home, but if I can put one queen of darkness under the sun before I die, then my ancestors won't be so ashamed of me anymore."

They carried the dealer into the van, tied him up and covered him with black tarp. The sun rose behind them, lighting up Table Mountain with a splendid gold as they drove back into Hope City proper. They didn't speak much on the way back. They knew they would need to rest after interrogating the dealer. Because they were gonna have a long night afterwards.

Chapter 10.Idleness

The last time I had been idle for an extensive length of time was long before my parents died. Since then, my life was abuzz with activity. Different homes, different caretakers, different schools. A new challenge every day. And no time to sit still. A hodgepodge of changing environments. Too fast to let me adjust and lie idle. Too fast to give me any time to think about what had happened to me. High school went quickly as I balanced living with Trudie or staying with my aunt when she was in town. Then I met Treth, became a monster hunter, and had even less time to do nothing. I was so busy for all these years, that I did not even stop to realise that I was busy. And throughout it all, the activity allowed me to never think about the hard stuff. Never enough time to brood.

But in the confines of Candace's keep, I had been inactive for weeks and, while I filled myself with the feverish anxiety of being contained in the territory of the enemy, I couldn't always hold onto this fear and anticipation. It didn't help that when Candace was around, which was rarely, she was usually quite pleasant. So long as we didn't discuss her necromancy, she was just like any teenage girl. In a way, she seemed more well-adjusted than

I did at her age. She cooked her own food, and more than just instant noodles, studied intensely, and ensured that she ate a balanced breakfast. That was when I saw her. Most of the time, my necromancer host was absent. I sometimes strayed close to her labs, and heard her working inside, but other times I couldn't find her anywhere. While I was limited to the halls of this dark keep, she had businesses to run. A necromantic empire to keep afloat. I didn't ask her about this or her magic. Not so much that I feared her reaction, but because I feared my own. I'm not one to hide my feelings and, as much as Candace intrigued me, with her air of innocence, I knew she engaged in the evil I had sworn to destroy. I chose to not think about it. I dare say that sometimes, when eating dinner with the strange little girl, while she roped me into conversations on music, fashion, literature and games, I couldn't help forgetting that she was a necromancer. In a way, I started to see her as a little sister.

I spent most of my days reading. There was no internet. No TV. No connection to the outside world. When I asked Candace in one of her rare appearances what was happening, she only shrugged. She wasn't paying attention. I suspected that the lack of internet and TV weren't to keep me isolated, but because Candace truly did not care about being connected to the outside world. Her empire was a means to an end. So long as she brought back her parents in her foolhardy experiments, she didn't care.

I read a lot in these weeks. I re-read *Warpwars*, caught up on a lot of the classics, and read some basic magic textbooks. Pranish would be proud. I even tried to incant some basic spells, but the local weyline was very odd. Treth and I suspected it to be a pure dark weyline, but it didn't feel like one. But neither did it feel right. It was like a flickering light-bulb. Constantly adjusting between light and dark. In a constant flux between good and evil. Perhaps, I couldn't help but wonder, like Candace herself. But that was hard to see. Besides what I knew she had done and some of her bouts of madness, she seemed…so normal.

Treth spent a lot of time discussing escape plans. I tended to shut them down. To his credit, he didn't suggest that we kill the girl. He was much too earnest for that, if a bit too narrow minded. But I knew he was right. We needed to escape. To kill Andy. Because Candace, for all my sister fantasies, was the enemy. Because I had been stuck here for weeks. Idle. And when I wasn't arguing with

Treth, talking to Candace or reading, I couldn't help but finally face what I have seen, and done.

My dreams were of my parents some nights. I woke up, shouting and sobbing. Treth consoled me until I fell back to sleep, exhausted. Other nights, I dreamed of Cornelius Black and Jeremiah Cox. I killed them again. Over and over. Sometimes, their faces changed as I shot and stabbed them. Sometimes to Trudie, sometimes to Pranish. Throughout the weeks, I killed Brett, Miriam, Cindy, Conrad, and even the image I had seen of Treth months ago. And most terrible of all, I saw myself killing Colin. Not even Treth could calm me down after those dreams. I came around with a scream and held my pillow over my face to keep myself silent, or to smother myself. Whatever came first. I tended to fall asleep and let go before I did myself any real harm.

Treth looked down at me. Sad. Sympathetic. But also, understanding. Years before, I would never show him this weakness. But we were...the same. In more than just body. He knew what I was going through. And that was why I could tolerate our disagreement about the girl necromancer.

On one night, through my restless throes of beckoning sleep, I finally gave up on rest and exited my cell-turned-room. I felt Treth in his chamber. While he didn't get physically tired, he confided in me that he did need some form of rest after so much sensory input and mental work. A form of meditation. After weeks watching over me in this place, I finally convinced him that he could afford to rest. If he thought Candace was a danger or not, it did not matter. He couldn't stop her and, if she was going to try something, she would have already.

I tiptoed through the dark halls, clearing my head as best I could, despite the oppressive blackness. I found the halls much less menacing with the knowledge that Candace wouldn't let me see her undead minions. I knew they were there, but at least I didn't have to see them. And I knew they weren't watching me. Only two things could be watching me. Petunia, the simple creature that Candace apparently created, and Candace herself. In my line of work, I could deal with that.

I made my way towards the kitchen, quietly so as not to alarm Treth or my fellow residents. I arrived at the kitchenette, with nothing but the faint lights of appliances to guide my way. I kept super quiet, as Candace's room was right next door. I didn't know if she was sleeping or not but didn't want to wake her if she was. Don't get me wrong. I'm not afraid of her! Honest. It's just…anybody could be scary if woken up abruptly. I know I would be pretty terrifying if someone disturbed my sleep.

While spreading peanut butter on bread in the darkness, I thought of Duer. He would often watch me as I made food. Sometimes I'd let him sample the food. He would then insult my cooking, just as he asked for more. I smiled, faintly and sadly. Where was he now? Was he okay? And who was looking after Alex? I stopped as I felt my heartbeat rise and had to lean against the counter. I missed them. All of them. And yet, I was also afraid to see them again. Because how soon would they end up dead because of their relationship to me?

I jumped as I heard the door to Candace's room open. A pool of light illuminated her as she rubbed her eyes. She was wearing light-blue pyjamas and her dark honey hair was loose and bedraggled around her head. Her eyes were half-closed as she let out a yawn.

I held my breath, as if I had awoken a bear in its cave. She was pleasant during the day, but I had no precedent for waking her. What would she do to me? I am ashamed to admit that I had lied. I was afraid.

"Kat?" she finally asked, hesitant, quiet. Like a mouse.

I felt Treth rouse himself and watch, curious. Hesitant. And, faintly, disgust. I could have shouted at him for feeling that way. She was just a little girl. In this dark room, watching her watching me with bleary eyes, I could not connect her to the Necrolord.

"Yes. It's me…" I said.

"I'm scared," she said, her voice breaking just a bit.

"Of what?" I asked, forgetting all about my midnight snack and the throbbing of my heart. My anxiety turned to curiosity, and subtly, to concern. Treth felt my concern and rolled his eyes.

Candace stepped further into the darkness. "I don't know…"

Her words were broken off by a sob.

My heart twisted, and I felt something I didn't understand, especially since I have never been overly fond of children. But even so, I saw this girl crying in the darkness, and I approached her, hesitantly.

"It's okay…Candy…there's nothing to be afraid of."

I didn't jump but was shocked all the same as she embraced me with a hug, nestling her head into my chest.

"You're wrong…" she said. "You're wrong."

I felt Treth watching me. Judging me. But something stronger told me what to do, and I put my arms around the scared little girl.

"Everything is okay. I'm here. Did you have a nightmare?"

"It's all a nightmare, Kat. All of it."

She hiccupped, and I felt moisture through my shirt as she cried. Was this truly the Necrolord? I knew it was, but I also realised something. It wasn't that simple.

"Can you stay with me tonight?" she asked, pleading, looking up, with eyes that could only belong to a child.

Before I could think it through, I answered.

"Of course, Candace."

Chapter 11. Birthday

There was a calendar in the kitchenette area that seemed to magically cross off each day as they passed. After some deep investigation, it was revealed to be as unmagical as a pre-Cataclysm slab of concrete. I was sure that Candace was the one marking down each day, but never actively saw her do it. Days ago, I awoke in her room, a small bedroom, half the size of my cell. She was gone. No word. No trace. She arrived again that evening, talking about a potato shortage like some sort of housewife or grocer. No mention of nightmares or my comforting her that night. I didn't talk about it. But what I did see was a glint in her eye. A sense of trust for me that only a child could have. The calendar said that night was three days ago and, as I ate peanut butter on toast, I saw an X through pen-written text on the wall calendar.

It was the 3rd of December 2036. And it was Candace's 15th birthday.

"I wonder how necromancers celebrate birthdays," Treth commented, bluntly.

I didn't like his tone. He had been grumpy for a long time. He didn't comment on me spending the night with

Candace, but I felt his displeasure. But what was I supposed to do?

Despite the calendar announcement, Candace was nowhere to be seen. I wondered if she'd be in her lab on her birthday but didn't want to look. I didn't like reminding myself of what she had in there.

I finished my toast and sat down in one of the armchairs. I was paging through *We the Living*. It had a slow start, but I was starting to get invested in the characters. As I began to become immersed in post-Revolutionary Russia, I heard a door creak. I looked up, expecting to see Candace.

The creature – Petunia – looked back at me, with its yellow eyes. It wasn't giggling. Rather, it looked expectant. This was the first time I had seen it since my initial introduction. I did sometimes hear it far off in the dark, however. Scurrying. Sometimes giggling. It gave me the creeps.

I maintained eye contact with the thing, as it slouched down in the door way, one hand on the floor and the other on the door handle, steadying itself.

"K-k-k…" it started sounding, and I was surprised to hear that its voice did not sound like that of an undead. No crackle of undead organs that should no longer be working. Not the deep rumble of magical verbalisation. It sounded...normal. The normal voice of a child. If an oddly proportioned, Tarzan wild-child. I had not noted before, as I did not make a habit of examining the clothing of the undead unless it was relevant to killing it, but the creature wore a floral print skirt and a blue t-shirt, with a picture of a Petunia on it.

Was this Candace's child?

Or just an experiment?

It was hard to tell with my girl necromancer host.

"K-k-kat..." Petunia managed to enunciate, and then grinned, extremely proud of it...herself.

I closed the book, marking my place with some folded-up scrap paper.

"What's up?" I asked, not knowing what else to say.

"Talking to monsters now, are we?" Treth snorted.

"I'm just being polite, Treth. And you heard Candace. It...she's alive. Some sort of artificial human."

"Necromancy is necromancy, Kat. It's a monster."

I stood up and Petunia's gaze followed me. She cocked her head as I looked at her, my eyebrow raised.

"Kat," she repeated. She pointed behind her and exited. I didn't follow, and she came back in, cocking her head.

"Kat," she repeated, more insistently.

"Alright," I said, and began following.

"Following monsters now, are we?" Treth sighed derisively.

"Do we have anything else to do?"

Treth didn't reply. Thought so!

Petunia led me, scurrying almost on all fours, around the crescent shaped hallway, past my room, and eventually to the dining room with the record player. Petunia disappeared inside, and I followed.

Fleetwood Mac was playing on the record player; the room was illuminated by cheerful fire and an assortment of candles. On the long dining room table was a large cake, covered with (on a quick count) 15 candles. Candace was sitting behind it, grinning ear to ear.

"Happy birthday," I said, instinctively and with almost the hint of a question in my voice. Candace didn't seem to notice my hesitation, as she stood up and gripped both my hands, almost dragging me to the table. She was positively buzzing with excitement. I took a seat and watched as Petunia awkwardly took a seat opposite me. She couldn't figure out the chair and ended up squatting on it. Candace didn't seem to mind.

"I'm so glad you could make it," Candace said, after taking a seat herself.

"I was in the area."

"This is my first birthday with someone at least close to my age in over 7 years," she said. "I wanted it to be special."

"What have you been doing for your birthdays for all those years?"

"For the first few, Igor attended…Mentor went to some. Then the Marshal…"

"I'm sorry," I said, instinctively. Sure, the Marshal was a murderous undead monstrosity but, in a way, I respected him. And by the sound of it, he had been a friend to Candace.

"It's fine. He was already dead," Candace waved away the comment, and then smiled. "And now you're here. And Petunia."

Petunia cocked her head and grinned. I winced as her long black dreads came awfully close to the fire.

"What would you do with the Marshal? On your birthdays, I mean."

"Talk, mostly," she said. "One year he got me a piñata, even though he's Portuguese and not Spanish. But I appreciated it all the same. I don't think he knew that I knew the difference."

"How…how was he?"

"The Marshal?" Candace pondered the question, the candle flames flickered, playing with the light. "He…liked to talk. Liked to listen. I liked him."

"Are you sure you're not…angry at me?"

"The Marshal wanted to fight you. It was his right." Candace shrugged. "You did what you had to do. But he brought you here to me."

"You know…" I started, trying my luck a bit. "That our deal didn't really entail you imprisoning me."

"Imprisoning?" she cocked her head. Petunia imitated her.

"Well, I'm not allowed to leave."

"You'll die if you leave."

I chuckled. "I've survived quite a long time and a lot worse. I'm sure I'd be alright."

Candace shook her head. "No, no. Much too unsafe. You're safer here with me. Where you can help me."

"Help you? How am I helping you?"

She smiled, faintly. "You just are."

She looked at the cake and then clapped her hands together to punctuate the conversation. She rubbed them together in anticipation.

"I ordered red velvet. I hope you like it!"

She didn't make a move, rather watching me intently. Awkwardly, I began speaking.

"Happy…birthday…to you…"

And, as Petunia started mouthing the words and Candace blushed in that way only natural for someone being sung to on her birthday, I began to sing properly, ending off with 15 claps and a hip-hip hooray.

Candace's face lit up with a smile and she blew out her candles. Two remained.

"Two boyfriends," I said, grinning myself and ignoring Treth's judgemental gaze and confusion at an Earthly practice he would never have witnessed until now. I had not gone to any of these sorts of parties with Treth.

Candace's cheeks turned a fierce red and she blew out the remaining two candles. She indicated for me to cut some pieces as she clasped her hands, grinning like an overexcited child. In a way, that's what she was.

I cut a piece for her, for myself, and for Petunia. Petunia considered the cake but, after seeing Candace stuff the entire piece into her mouth, did the same. I couldn't help but laugh, causing Candace to look up quizzically, and then laugh too, her cheeks full and frosting coating her lips.

I hadn't had red velvet cake in ages. Trudie's sixteenth birthday. Pranish had to leave early after his parents called him. That had really upset him. He didn't get to see Trudie's excitement when she unwrapped the copy of *Corsairs of Duty 6* that he got her. In hindsight, he really overspent on her. But who could blame him? He was a rich kid devoted to a girl he was too timid to ask out.

I hoped they were okay.

Candace must have noticed my reverie, as she looked at me.

"Something wrong with the cake?"

"No, no…it's great…" I said, trying to give a half-hearted smile. I failed.

"What's wrong?"

How could I tell her? My archnemesis. My host. A young girl.

"I miss my friends," I said, simply.

"Aren't we friends?" she asked, a hint of desperation and uncertainty in her voice.

Were we friends? I didn't know. Treth wouldn't really consent to it. But he wasn't my boss. But with what she had done…

"Yeah," I answered, not knowing if it was a lie or not, "But I can have more than one friend. And I don't even know what happened to them."

"They're alive," she said, simply.

"Not all of them," I grumbled.

She cocked her head. That was where Petunia must get it from. Such an odd thing for a human to do, but like when dogs did it, it was somehow endearing.

"That man. The one with glasses. What was he?"

What was he? A man I loved. Still loved. But he was dead.

Fuck. What was I doing here? And why didn't I cry?

"I loved him," I said, surprised that I said it out loud.

"Did the vampires kill him?"

"No…" I said, and my fist tightened on the table top. "A werewolf did. Someone I used to like. But not any fucking more. And that's why I need to leave. I have to kill him."

"I could kill him for you." She said it like one would suggest offering someone a lift to the airport. But in this respect, I didn't actually mind.

"No…I have to do it."

"What if…if you could bring back…"

"Colin," I offered, and shook my head. "No. Not possible. As much as Petunia is impressive…"

The creature grinned at her name.

"She's not the same as resurrecting the dead. You can animate a corpse, but the soul…necromancy has no dominion over the soul. At this stage, I think it's even too late to bring him back as a wight…"

I winced at the thought of Colin as a wight. I could not do that to him. Or myself.

"Do you know when the Marshal died?" Candace asked.

"24 hours before his reanimation is all I can say," I grumbled as I bit on another piece of cake. Creating wights wasn't something the necromancers tried to do on purpose, but sometimes the soul clung to a corpse within a day of its death. Wilful souls would find their way back into reanimated bodies, becoming wights.

"He died 200 years before his resurrection by a necromancer - that he promptly killed. He had not consented to coming back, you see. The necromancer cabals say it was a fluke, apparently. A wight, as you said, must be reanimated within 24 hours of death, or else the soul is unreachable. Yet, his soul clung to his corpse for 200 years, awaiting his return."

I didn't reply. It sounded impossible to me. Necromancy had rules. Sure, I didn't know all of them, but I knew enough. More than any damn Puretide operative, that's for sure.

"He spoke a lot about his life," Candace said. "Probably to you as well. You spoke for awhile before your duel, it looked like."

She must have watched me kill him. Her friend. What did that make her? What did that make me?

"He died during the Portuguese age of exploration and was then embalmed and entombed in Lisbon. Usually, the soul escapes the body and never comes back. But, something kept his soul there, or…" her eyes lit up. "Brought it back."

"Even so, being a wight isn't like being alive again. You said so yourself. Colin can't come back."

He can't.

He was gone.

They were gone.

All gone.

"That is why I don't only study necromancy," she said, proudly. "But healing, too."

I scoffed. "Impossible. The dark and light weyline energy would cancel each other out."

I said that, but then thought about the fluxes in the local weyline. Light and dark. Simultaneously.

"When the darkness is put into servitude, it fights back," Candace said, business-like, sounding more like a scholar than the previous child talking with her mouth full. "But it can't fight forever. Eventually, it tires out. When it does, I can heal. Alchemy also helps. With the right reagents, I can circumvent the need for a constantly light weyline. And that's how I plan to bring my parents back. The dark, the light, the ancient sciences, and the new sciences."

She stared at me earnestly. I didn't respond. Eventually, she lost interest and stood up to change the record. Petunia was done with her slice of cake and reached out towards the knife. I watched as she stretched out with her gangly arm, black hair covering one of her eyes. She tried to grab the knife by the blade and cut herself, bleeding red blood onto the table. She cried out. Impulsively, I reached forward to check the damage. And she sank her teeth into my arm. I yelled and gripped the creature by the throat. My heart stopped, and I felt an intense, searing sensation through my veins. Like coal in my arteries. I had felt it before. The sensation stopped, and I fell backwards, onto the ground, watching Petunia scurry away.

She had red blood. Human blood. She was alive.

"I'm so sorry!" Candace sobbed, caught between a shout and a whine. "I didn't want to…but you did this. Why?! My birthday…"

A trail of blood led outside of the room.

I slowly lifted myself up. Candace was clutching her head with both hands. Her expression was pained.

"My head. It hurts! Why won't the pain go away. Please."

She looked at me, with eyes that I couldn't tell if I should pity or fear.

"Help me please. Help me make it go away."

I stood, backing away slowly as she pulled out pieces of hair.

"You ruined it. No! I ruined it. The pain! MAKE IT STOP!"

My back was to the door, the one leading to my room. Candace opened her hazel eyes and looked at me pleadingly.

"Please…don't go."

I almost didn't reach for the door handle, until she screamed, and I ran for it.

"You see now, Kat?" Treth said, with no hint of smugness. Just sad resignation. Did I misjudge him? Did he also pity her?

"She's not a child. Anymore, at least. She's dangerous. For both our sakes, we need to leave."

As uncertain as I had been before, now I agreed.

Chapter 12. Escape

Treth was right. We had to leave. The problem was that I hadn't been concentrating on how I should escape. But while I may have been uncertain about Candace and my place in the world these past weeks – probably even a month now – Treth, always the knight with a plan, had been plotting our escape.

We had not found an entrance or exit to our expansive abode, despite the fact that we knew there had to be one. We had entered, after all. And Candace left regularly, meaning there must be some way of getting in and out. But even if we were to find it, we felt that going through the door she used was a bad idea. Treth had a better idea.

"I felt it the first time we were in the freezers."

"The only time," I corrected him.

"It had more airflow than any other room. Had to have it. The heat has to go somewhere. And we can breathe. Which means vents."

"You've been watching too many movies."

"That means you have as well. Anyway, if we can find a way into the vents, it has to go somewhere. And that somewhere has to go outside."

I didn't respond, rather choosing to frown as I lay down on the bed of my cell/room, the metal door closed and bolted from my side. I hadn't seen Candace since her episode of madness earlier today. I had chosen to stay in my room and hadn't been hungry enough to come out for dinner.

"Kat…" Treth pleaded. "You don't seem serious about this. Are you still…"

I didn't let him finish the sentence. "No. Go on. I'm listening."

Treth examined me, sceptical, but he continued.

"I believe the necromancer does trust you, which means I am not anticipating resistance. But, just in case, see if you can conceal one of the kitchen knives."

"To do what?!" I shouted, suddenly. Shocking both Treth and myself.

Finally, he answered.

"To…to kill any undead she sends your way."

"Oh…okay."

"Kat…I know she looks fragile. I know she…reminds you of…"

"She doesn't remind me of anyone," I lied, cutting him off. "We won't need a knife. Let's…"

I hesitated, and sat up in my bed, shaking my head.

"Let's just go," I finally whispered.

I felt some initial worry from my spirit companion, but then a nod.

"Go through the dining room," he said. "To avoid her bedroom."

"What if she's still there?"

"Then we delay."

I creased my forehead. I was sure it wasn't that simple. If I saw her again, what would I think about what I was planning? Would I reconsider this escape plan? What would Treth think about me then? And would I care?

It should have been simple! I wasn't supposed to feel this way about the enemy.

No, I had to rip the bandaid off fast. No more pitying necromancers and monsters. I had to get out of here. To see if my friends were okay. And to kill Andy.

With that purpose-filled thought, I left my room. The hall was always silent, but it felt eerily more so. The calm after the storm. Where was Candace now? Out of the stronghold, cooling off, I hoped.

After I escaped, what would she do? Would she come after me again? Or would she find someone else? And if either me or another, would the massacres resume? Or did they even stop?

I snuck up to the door to the dining room and listened. Nothing but the looping scratch of the record player. I opened the door. Bloody droplets from Petunia's hand, smashed cake and tossed records were all that remained of the party. No Candace. I could have breathed a sigh of relief, yet I couldn't help but feel a sense of worry over what had happened to her.

The hall on the other side of the dining room was darker than I remembered. I navigated by the faint outlines of the curving corridor, leading towards a blue-tinged light in the distance. I felt cold from the light. I stopped at the door.

The lab revealed the extent of Candace's evil. I knew that. I just didn't want to believe it. I didn't want to believe that the little girl that I had to comfort at night collected the eyes, heads and organs of her victims. I didn't want to think that someone so young could have embraced the darkness so readily. But above all, I didn't want her to be right.

For if she could bring back her parents, then that meant I could have. And if it was possible, did I really choose the right side?

I opened the door to the lab, holding my breath to avoid the acrid smell of rot and reagents but, as I entered, I saw nothing. The experiments, corpses, body-parts and necro-widgets were all gone. All that was left were clean countertops, sanitised surgery tools, and empty jars. It could have passed for a new campus laboratory or even a cafeteria.

It had been a long time since I was last in the lab. When did this all happen?

"It all may be gone now, but don't forget that it was here in the first place," Treth said, sternly. I nodded. I knew Treth was right. No matter my feelings on the matter, Candace was the Necrolord. My enemy. She had created the abomination. Her zombies bit Hammond. Drake was killed investigating HER. I couldn't be here anymore. I needed fresh air. I needed the open sky.

I made my way through the sterilised laboratory to the double doors leading to the freezer. A gust of icy wind met me on my way in.

I stopped and listened. I didn't hear any footsteps, talking, or crying. Nothing but the faint hum of the freezers. With Treth helping, we navigated through the halls, never going into any of the side freezers. I knew what they contained, and I didn't want to see them, even if the sight of hundreds of frozen corpses may have confirmed my reasons for leaving. And in a big way, I didn't want to confirm what I already knew. I wanted Candace to be that fragile little girl who needed me to keep away the nightmares. But I also knew that I could not be that person. She was a necromancer. I hunted necromancers. And even if she was a normal child, tenderness was not my domain. Perhaps, I found a sense of solace in comforting a child. A comfort knowing that, at least a bit of me, was still kind and human. But it was not a comfort I could allow myself. I had too many things to do. Too many things to kill. My life did not allow for softness and I had to be hard as I escaped my prison, no matter how homely it may have started to feel.

Treth heard the hum as I felt the increased flow of air. We looked up and allowed our vision to adjust. The vent cover was the same colour as the ceiling, but we could see its outline.

"A little bit of a jump," I whispered.

"You've made larger jumps before. My worry is how to get it dislodged."

"One way to find out."

I bent my knees, and jumped, reaching towards the vent. My fingertips brushed centimetres away from the ceiling and I felt the cold air of the outside world coming through.

"Almost," Treth commented. "It's a good thing you're so tall…for a girl."

"If you're trying out some infantile humour now, I'd stop while you're ahead. I'm pretty sure I'm taller than you."

Treth didn't respond, but I felt his cheeks redden. Boys!

I backed off a bit from the vent and took a running jump. My fingers felt an indentation and I clasped my hand, holding onto the grating, with my feet dangling. The edge of my hand-hold bit into my skin and I winced. Then suddenly, relief, as the vent fell to the ground, clanging even as I felt and heard a thud and my own "oof" of pain.

"Seems it was loose. Do you think it's large enough for you to fit inside?"

"Another joke?" I asked, my backside stinging from my fall.

"No. Genuine question. Vents aren't designed for humans. Not often."

I looked up, squinting. The darker patch in the ceiling, uncovered now, seemed large enough. Must have been intentionally made for someone to crawl through for maintenance purposes. Admittedly, I did not know much about the mysteries of building repair.

"Think she would have heard that?" I asked, indicating the fallen vent.

"Not unless she's in these tunnels," he replied. "Sound seems to stop at the doors. But best we hurry. Just in case."

I nodded and stood, rubbing my injuries. I was going have a nasty bruise.

I took another running jump and gripped the edge of the vent-hole. I lifted myself up with a bit of strain, but it seemed that, despite my recent laziness, I was still in shape. The vent itself was small, triggering any latent claustrophobia I may have had. While I could fit, I had to crawl along on my stomach, not knowing which direction to go. I picked directions that felt right and crawled, meeting dead-ends with vents to other parts of the same floor. Through slats, I saw flesh-puppets, idle and standing in their rooms. I didn't rush, for risk of catching their attention. If they noticed me, Candace would. I turned back and continued the criss-cross of ventilation shafts, building a sweat that ran down my face and stung my eyes. My hair, grown longer and loose, fell all over the place, with strands sticking to my face. My arms and legs chafed. My knees hurt. No. Everything hurt. My energy was fading, but I kept crawling, in a semi-conscious state. I couldn't turn back. Not with Treth and not after the attempt. I had to get out.

The sound of cars hooting, people shouting, and alarms ringing gave me pause. I suspected that Candace's stronghold would be more isolated. But this sounded like a city. I got a whiff of burning rubber and trash, mixed with the pungent smell of petrol. It was not just the city. It was the slums.

It made sense. Candace's empire was built within the slums. It was only right for her stronghold to be in the centre of it all. Even so, I kept unconsciously trying to disconnect Candace from the Necrolord. The ease of doing so was worrisome. If I had to, would I be able to kill her? The thought horrified me and I continued the crawl.

Pain became excruciating, my eyes involuntarily closed as my mind dozed, even as I kept crawling, pulling myself inch by painful agonising inch, until I hit the end of the road, and the rest of the vent went up.

Oh, Athena! Rifts! And the fucking In-Between. I couldn't do it. No more. I had been in these vents for hours. It felt like days. I had breathed in all manner of dust, smoke and my own expended CO_2. My vision was faint enough that I could have fallen asleep, despite the metal all around me. Pressing in. Baking me like sweaty bread. Crushing me. Crushing my spirit.

But a voice in my head, not Treth's, but my own, told me to keep moving. I looked up and saw light. Treth watched me with concern, pity, guilt and anticipation. I slowly lifted my body into the vertical shaft and pressed my hands to the sides. I tried to lift my weight, but I couldn't. It felt like I was trying to lift the Titan Citadel. I felt Treth's trust in me. His confidence that I would succeed, but it wasn't him who kept me going. It was the other voice, that told me that I couldn't stop.

I pressed my hands tighter against my metal confines, and lifted myself up, then pressed my shoes against the sides. The strain was too much, and I stopped. The rubber soles of my shoes squeaked as they slipped. The voice didn't let me stop. It didn't allow me reprieve. And I listened. And despite my grunts, and panting, I kept on going. Slowly, slowly, I rose. Between squeaks, the screeching of metal and my laboured breaths. Until I could smell the slums and feel the air.

I curled myself up into a ball, still pressing myself between the shaft walls, and kicked towards the light. I almost fell as the grating gave way. I grabbed on and pulled myself through.

Despite all the stench, it smelled wonderful. It smelled genuine. I was free.

The light peeking through the vent had been from the moon and a large billboard advertising hard liquor to those who could not afford it but bought it anyway. And despite the reek of poverty and decay, I took in a deep breath, stood up outside the vent and held my arms out, absorbing it all. I did not know until now how hard my confinement had been. Humans were not meant to be caged and even the most misanthropic hermit needed air and nightsky.

I took it all in. The distant gunfire, the shouts of hawkers, the backfire of cars, the smell of booze, shit and rubber, and the sight of a sea of lights around me.

I now understood what the archdemon had been talking about, what seemed a lifetime ago, even if it was just a few months.

This was life.

Unpleasant. Pleasant. Ordered. Chaotic. Shit or wonderful. It was life. And I had missed it.

I grounded myself as I felt Treth's impatience. He was not as awed as I. I looked at our surroundings and found that we were on top of a rather tall building.

"Seems we were incorrect about it being underground," I said.

"Perhaps it is best to hide in plain sight. Or maybe the Necrolord doesn't need to hide at all."

"I find that hard to believe, seeing as Drake never tracked her down. In fact, I don't think we ever raided this area."

"Hope City is a large place. Larger than any city in my world. I do not hope to experience it all, for I believe it would take both our lifetimes and more."

I nodded, a bit forlornly. It was not like I wanted to experience all of Hope City. The majority of it was a sprawl of slums, after all. But missing out on any experience, there was a sense of loss.

"We should start thinking of a way to get…"

"Kat…"

A voice I strongly hoped I wouldn't hear cut me off.

I spun on my heels to see Candace, lit up by the billboard, standing by an open doorway.

I turned to run.

"Please…don't go." It must have been something in her tone that made me stop. A fragility. It wasn't a command. And it wasn't a whine. It was a childlike plea. From someone so desperate that they would do anything to not be hurt again.

Dammit it! I still pitied her. Like a victim. Like a little sister.

Treth shouted at me. "Run! Don't listen to her."

"Kat, please…" Candace pleaded again. Still not a whine. A sincere plea. Mature, yet childlike all the same. But more than that, despairing. What would happen to her if I left?

"I will change. I'm doing my best. I can get better. Please. Stay with me. You're the only thing that makes me feel safe."

"But what about the people you killed?" I burst out, turning on my heels to face her. "They can't feel safe anymore. The people you tortured. Reanimated. That abomination. The zombies. The friends of mine you've murdered. Am I meant to forget about that? To go on cuddling with you so you won't have nightmares? You're not a child, Candance. You're a necromancer. You create monsters. You're...you're like the man who killed my parents. How can I forget that? How can I be friends with you when you represent everything I hate?"

Thematically, the surrounding noise of the slum seemed to stop, as Candace looked at me, stunned. Her eyes showed contemplation, but the quiver of her lip showed how much I must have really gotten to her.

"I'm trying to get better," she repeated, almost a whisper. She looked me in the eyes, and despite her tears, her boldness impressed even me. "I know what I've done. And I know I should feel guilty for doing it. And I will. One day. But before that day comes, I need you. I need you to be with me because you're the only one who knows how I feel, and the only one who can truly fathom how important my project really is."

"I can't, Candace," I said, shaking my head sadly, but sternly. "I have to go. I can't stay locked up in there while my friends are out here. While this whole world is out here. I need to get back to my work. I have people to kill. Your goals and my goals are not the same. My parents are dead. They aren't coming back."

She didn't reply, but the pain in her eyes was answer enough. A look of loss so deeply felt it was as if I was dying.

"Okay, Kat…" she finally said, meekly. "I think…I think I understand. I will try to hold the madness away. So, you can get away. I will. But…but…"

She withdrew a knife. A large stainless-steel kitchen knife.

"Kat…please kill me."

Taken aback, I took a step away. I felt Treth's shock coalesce with mine.

"What?!" was all I could blurt out.

"The darkness beckons me, Kat. It does not only want to lend its power to me in short bursts any more. It wants me. Entirely. But I will not be its slave. Please, kill me. If I can't bring back my parents, then I may as well be dead. And without you, I know I won't. If I don't die here, then I will keep making monsters, and the darkness will consume me too much for me to bring back my parents properly."

I looked at the knife, and finally, shook my head. I felt Treth's dismay. He didn't understand why I couldn't do it. Why I couldn't kill Candace, even if she wanted me to. He couldn't understand.

She was me.

"I can't, I'm sorry."

I turned to leave, even as I heard the thud of her knees hit the roof as she fell. Between choked sobs, she cried.

"I'm trying to get better…please, believe me. Don't go. I need you. Please!"

And I heard the hint of madness come into her voice.

"I'll show you, Kitty Kat! I'll bring them back. I'll be with them again."

And sanity again.

"Don't let it take me. Please. Please!"

Please. Please. Please.

Please. Please.

Please.

I stopped, my feet on the precipice of the roof.

"Kat, what are you doing?" Treth asked.

I turned back to Candace, even as she balled her eyes out. She stopped, with only a few sniffles, as I placed my hand on her head.

"Let's go inside," I said, and helped guide Candace back into the stronghold, even as Treth screamed at me that I was lost to the darkness.

Chapter 13.Sanguine

The last time Brett had seen Miriam LeBlanc, she had been smiling. Nothing so unrefined as a toothy grin, but rather a subtle and satisfied curve of the lip. Brett had thought at the time that Miriam looked like a vampire, but he had enough sense to know that Miriam, despite her dark fashion and pallid skin, looked much too old to be a vampire. Rather, her appearance seemed to be an unconscious imitation of her dedicated study. Fashion was very much a cultural phenomenon, and culture is just a case of mass imitation. Miriam spent most of her time around vampires. So, the only things she had to imitate were goth wannabes with a blood-based diet.

Miriam was not smiling now.

"Conrad told me what you're doing," she said, her tone measured, even as she clenched her fists. Brett and Guy divided their attention between her and their equipment on the table. Most of it was ready, but there were some last-minute checks that needed to be made before nightfall. Brett and Guy didn't mind Miriam seeing their less than legal arsenal. Friends of Conrad seldom coloured in the lines of the law. And both Brett and Guy had enough favours with the cops that they could probably get away with owning a tank.

That was something Kat didn't get. Sure, the cops and bureaucrats were often scummy, incompetent and lazy, but they set the rules. If you wanted to play the game, you had to schmooze. Had to make friends. Had to actually play the game. No point calling every cop a tick. Best it accomplished was pissing them off. Brett and Guy disliked Hope City's less-than-finest just as much as the next private contractor, but the cops didn't need to know that. And drinks were cheap. Bringing coffee to a clean-up for a Council call-out cost a few bucks and meant that everyone there felt they owed you something when push came to shove. Give it a few years, and every bit of coffee, donuts, and pro-bono monster hunting work meant that precincts looked the other way while you committed mass murder.

Brett and Guy were also not worried about Miriam going to the cops with the information that Conrad had given her. If she had any intention of doing so, then there'd be cops at the door, not her.

"You know more about vampires than we do," Guy answered her. "And that's why you're here and not cops."

"Vampires are monsters," she said, pointing out the obvious to Brett and Guy. "But so is the kraken and dragons. Yet, we don't hunt them with impunity."

"Dragons and krakens don't kill as many humans as vampires do," Brett replied.

She shook her head. "Proportionately, krakens and dragons kill insurmountably more than vampires."

"Statistics is a demonic language," Guy replied. "Please cut to the chase. If you might not have guessed, we're planning on heading out tonight."

Her pale cheeks reddened, confirming that she wasn't a vampire. She looked about to yell but closed her eyes and sighed heavily.

"You're going after Victoria Kruger of the Sanguineas Syndicate. Tonight."

"If anyone knows who has Kat, she does. And that's if the bitch-vampire doesn't have Kat herself," Brett replied, focusing most of his attention on a quite illegal sub-machine gun. The silver hollow-points for it had cost a fortune, but they were needed to put down fledglings quickly. Wouldn't do much against any hardier strains. The shotgun and axe would have to work for that.

"You know what she is?" Miriam asked, aghast. "She's not some two-bit vampire gangster. She's the head of the oldest vampire syndicate on the continent. She rules over hundreds, if not thousands, of vampires. The Zulu Vampire cabals even give her a wide berth."

"I've fought true vamps before, LeBlanc," Brett said. "I'll fight her. And she'll tell me how to find Kat."

"You realise what has happened to Kat if the vampires did take her, right?"

Brett chose to ignore her. It couldn't be true. Not Kat. She had fought the Ancients themselves. She wouldn't let herself be turned.

"Kruger is not just any post-Cataclysm vampire, Callahan," Miriam continued, using Brett's rarely heard surname. "She's defeated true vampires. Consumed them. And somehow, she's managed to control her own mutations. She's powerful. Too powerful for you measly mortals. It is by her own remnants of humanity, I think, that she hasn't taken over this city."

"She lives in a manor in the suburbs. She gets her daily blood. She sends errand boys to buy red dresses," Guy recounted. "Doesn't sound like some eldritch monster to me. Just a vamp-lord."

He indicated the ensemble of weapons on the table.

"We've dealt with vamp-lords. We'll be fine."

She shook her head, almost viciously.

"I also want Kat to be found. But this isn't the way. This is suicide! But I can see that you are too blinded by your hatred for blood-suckers. But you should have learnt by now that hatred doesn't win wars. Cold, calculating reasoning does. I don't hate vampires. Because if I did, I wouldn't be able to understand them. I would be consumed by rage, and then do something stupid like this."

She gestured at the arsenal on the table top and then turned her back.

"Goodbye. And if I see you two again, I hope you don't have fangs."

Guy shut the door behind her and they wordlessly got back to their preparations.

***

They attacked at night. Usually, they would attack a vamp compound during the day, but the Sanguineas headquarters was an odd case. During the day, the house was full of off-duty vamps. Sure, they'd be tired. Some would even be sleeping. Human habits were hard to break.

But most would be wide awake, watching TV in the dark, discussing their kills, or doing whatever humans-turned-monsters did in their time off. If Guy and Brett attacked during the day, they'd find themselves face to face with a manor full of very angry, if groggy, vampires. The night, on the other hand, saw the manor at its quietest. Only a few guards and lieutenants. And hopefully, the boss herself.

The sun had set and the night air was cool in Constantia. Leafy suburb is often just a saying, but Constantia is properly leafy. Mansions were interspersed with lush forests, rivers and horse tracks, all in the shadow of Table Mountain. It had a clean and strong weyline, protected by hidden fae and strictly enforced property rights. It was a place for old money and the rich who did not want to be seen. For a vampire, it would also help that the trees and high peaks created an unassailable shadow. Night was longer in Constantia.

Brett hid in the brush, opposite Kruger's manor. While any vamp that knew he was there would be able to see him, he was betting on their apathy more than any flaw in their senses. Guy was waiting in the brush somewhere else, standing by for Brett to make the first move. Brett knew it was because he was the close combat specialist. The man in front. But he hated it. Not the danger for himself. The Corps knocked that sort of selfish thought out of its recruits quickly. No. Brett hated being the one to start the assault because it meant he was the one who ultimately condemned his team to death. It was his job to start the mission. And if someone died during the mission that he started, then at least some of the blame was on him.

Brett knew that Guy was ready to die. And that made it worse. But he also knew that he did not have the right to deny his friend a shot at vengeance against the evil that had scarred them both.

This wasn't just about Kat, Brett had to admit to himself. She had been the reason to start slaying again but, once they had started, they realised that this was their purpose. Their drive. When they killed vampires, the nightmares stopped, and they could breathe again. It was their reason for being.

Brett exhaled softly. The night was dark, with only the occasional streetlight and a single white lamp by the wrought-iron fence. A guard hut, manned during the day by a human security guard, sat next to the lamp. It was empty now.

Vampires owned the night. At least, that's what they thought. Brett and Guy had proven so many of them wrong. They would prove them wrong again.

An engine started in the distance and Brett watched as a car drove up to the gate from the inside. It didn't have its lights on. Vampires wouldn't need lights. A man got out and opened the gate. Brett watched, despite the limited lighting, how the gate was locked with a simple padlock and chain. Very lax security.

Once the car drove onto the main street, it turned on its lights, for the benefit of more human drivers. Once the sound of its engine faded away, Brett hurried across the street, a pair of bolt cutters in one hand and a sawed-off in the other. He took cover by the side of the gate. Listened. Silence.

He holstered his gun and heard scurrying from the bushes. Guy appeared on the other side of the gate. Brett nodded and placed the jaws of the bolt cutter on the padlock. With a tight squeeze, it broke open. Guy lifted the chains as quietly as possible as Brett put away the cutters and drew his two-handed pump-action shotgun. He chambered a round and took the lead.

The road up to Kruger's mansion was also dark. Driveway lined with trees. Must look nice during the day. Green avenue. Looked like a haunted forest from an old Disney film at night. The branches looked like monsters grabbing at them in the dark. Brett and Guy stuck to the road. If the vampire could see them on the driveway, they could see them in the trees. So, might as well use the road and be a bit faster about it.

Kruger's mansion was not what Brett expected. There were two types of homes that rich vampire lords tended to acquire. Either, an old and stereotypical gothic manor house to go with the image, or an opulent and gaudy modern design to show off their newfound wealth and power. Kruger's was neither. It was a contemporary suburban design. Pitched roof. Simple frames. Nothing over the top. Sure, it was large. But not as large as some other monstrosities built in the area. It could have easily fit into any suburb in Hope City. The windows were unshuttered, and some were open. Brett would bet money on it that there were automatic metal shutters on every window to keep out the sun during the day. They would have to be careful about that when thinking about their escape.

The almost normalcy of the Kruger manor was one thing, but even more peculiar was the fact that the front door was wide-open, with faint candlelight from within silhouetting the doorway.

Brett and Guy shared a look of bemusement. Vampires, especially young vampires, could be careless. Brett and Guy thrived off careless vampires. But Kruger, queen of Sanguineas, was not careless. They had to remember that.

Brett took point and Guy followed. They flanked the door and peered in. Melting candles stood on a table in the entry-hall, lighting up a photo of a young woman with dark brown hair. Bouquets of red flowers adorned the floor around the table. Brett had heard descriptions of Violetta Kruger's appearance and this was not a photo of her. And it didn't look like a shrine. Rather, the sort of thing you'd see at a funeral. Brett didn't recognise the girl in the picture. He was sure it wasn't one of his kills.

From a doorway further in, they could hear the crackle of burning logs and see the warm orange-red glow of a fireplace. It was summer this time of year in the southern hemisphere, but Constantia still got pretty cold. And vampires didn't really care about temperature. The ambience of a fire could be had without the discomfort of a boiling room.

There were plenty of things to note in the entry-hall, but above all was the distinct lack of vampires. Brett placed his finger on the trigger, ready to fire instantaneously, and entered. He felt Guy's reassuring presence behind him as they moved into the room. Besides the crackle of the fire and a distant wind through the trees, the house was silent. No voices. Not even the habitual breathing that many fledgling vampires maintained. No sign of life. Cursed or uncursed.

Was their intel incorrect? Was Kruger not here? Brett couldn't help but feel equal parts relief and disappointment that their kill had got away. He still kept his shotgun aloft, aiming it at every doorway as he walked softly. The floor creaked under his boot. And the candles flickered out and the glow of the fire turned to black. Everything went dark. Only a lifetime of drilling and experience stopped Brett and Guy from physically jumping from shock.

They could hear nothing now. Nothing except for the beating of their hearts. They tried to search for an opening. An enemy. Something to shoot at. But they could see nothing. Only years of discipline held them back from opening fire, lest they shoot one another.

Through the darkness, previously empty, a presence appeared. Not from any particular direction. But as if the house was alive.

"Hunters. Slayers in the dark," a voice, predatory and feminine, purred. "It has been too long since humans entered my nest without permission."

Brett turned and saw a pair of red eyes staring back.

"Too long," it whispered, licking its lips.

Brett fired point-blank, lighting up an empty room. Where was Guy? Where was the vampire?

The voice laughed.

"Silver-shot. Silver axe. Silver blade. An arsenal to slay blood-suckers. You come prepared, human. But I would not expect any less from one bearing the numbers of the...Corps..."

She trailed off at the last word and Brett felt someone standing behind him. He drew his axe with a flourish and lashed out, stopping just as he saw Guy's eyes, wild with fright, and his pistols pointed at Brett's head. They stopped and turned, back to back.

"The house is empty, my uninvited guests. My children and associates have gone out to absorb the holiday. Why not you? It is almost sad for you to be skulking in the darkness of another's home, when you could be celebrating this most hallowed Christmas Eve at your own."

The room lit up, as if by moonlight, yet all the windows were now shuttered. It was as if the shadows had merely moved away, to hide in the corners and under the furniture.

"I choose to celebrate human holidays alone," the voice that Brett presumed to be Kruger herself, announced. "But company isn't the worst thing in the world."

A wall turned into a stairway in the blink of an eye and every other doorway and window became cream wallpaper.

"Odder things have occurred in this world than two vampire hunters and a vampire sharing a Christmas Eve," Kruger said, a hint of humour in her voice. "Come forward and let me tell you a story."

Without any other choice, Brett and Guy scaled the phantom staircase, holding their weapons for a false sense of reassurance.

"In the days after the Vortex opened and the Titan started to wake, vampires came to Hope City. One such vampire turned me, and I killed him for it. Shaken by what I had become, I sought solitude, only taking blood when the hunger drove me to madness. And in these bouts of madness, I killed many innocents. I drained children dry. Eviscerated their parents. I was a monster. Am still a monster. But, after every bit of feeding, when my hunger was sated, I gained lucidity…"

Brett felt a cold hand on the back of his neck. He turned and saw nothing. But in front of him, he saw the pair of red-eyes, growing further and further away.

"I saw what I had done," Kruger continued. "I saw the blood on my hands and felt the sweetness on my lips. But I also saw what my fellow vampires, so new to a world that had never truly known vampires before, were going through. The hunger. The madness. They were as much in pain as I was. Yet, we tried to maintain our humanity. Ironic, isn't it? That by feeding, by being monsters, we realised we wanted to be human."

She laughed, but her laugh held no humour.

"But we could never be human."

Guy indicated a doorway at the top of the staircase. Brett kicked it down and levelled his shotgun at a seemingly empty room. No furniture. No vampires. Nothing.

"But there was the problem. We tried to be human. The Spirit of the Law even acknowledged that we were human. Just…afflicted. Cursed."

Brett and Guy continued down the hall. There were no shadows. Just the dim light of a fictitious moon. And no sound but Kruger's voice inside their heads.

They heard footsteps. They turned and saw ghouls. Tens of them, sprinting at them from down the hall. Brett fired but his bullets didn't stop the tide. The ghouls hit them. And dissipated into smoke. An illusion. Shaken, they turned back down the hall and listened for the voice.

"But this is more than just an affliction, hunters. And you know this. It is a great irony that the only humans who truly understand us are our enemies. They understand that we aren't humans anymore. We aren't something that can be cured. Or saved. And neither do we truly belong in human society."

A face, pale and feminine, appeared just before Brett's. A handspan away. He tried to cry out, but nothing escaped his lips. The face was that of a young woman's, with a pointed nose, almond-shaped red eyes, blonde hair in a bun and secretary glasses. She smiled, revealing two glistening fangs. Brett simultaneously found her gorgeous and the most horrific thing he had ever seen.

He tried to lift his weapons, but his body was frozen, even as Kruger circled him and embraced him from behind, squeezing his chest and groin. He felt warm breath on his neck and felt the cold, hard caress of a fang consider his neck.

She laughed and shoved him onto the ground. At the same time, Brett saw Guy shoved to the floor as well.

"We are monsters. And that is the simple crux of this disjointed tale. We are blood-hungry beasts. And I am their queen. But this is where you have misunderstood me…"

The lightning in the room suddenly turned to the natural yellow glow of a bulb, coming from a light-stand on a mahogany desk. Kruger sat on the side of the desk, considering the two men prostrate on the floor.

"I keep the monsters in line," she said, simply. "Yet, you want to kill me? The Corps at its height could not stop the vampire cartels from destroying the north, yet you expect the two of you to police this city from my people?

You remove me, if you even can, and this city will die. It will be drained of every last drop. This is not a threat. But a certainty. I keep the monsters from breaking your precious civilisation, so they can feed every day instead of one drunken night of blood-filled revelry."

Brett lifted his shotgun and aimed it at the vampire before him. Her eyes were laughing. He pulled the trigger. Click.

She grinned as she pulled a shotgun shell out of her pocket.

"Where..." Brett said, between panting and confusion. "Is Kat Drummond?"

She laughed.

"Is that what this is about? A two-bit monster slayer?"

"You have her!" Brett yelled, finding some of his courage. "Give her back!"

"Or else? You aren't in a position to be making threats, Corpsman."

"We've got friends. They'll tear the ceiling off every stronghold you have. You will never be able to hide from the sun ever again."

"Stop being silly," she said, chastising a child. "And take an actual seat. You look unseemly."

Hesitantly, Brett and Guy stood. Brett considered reaching for his axe or knife, but seeing the nonchalant way that Kruger crossed her bare white legs while sitting on her table made him realise how impotent he really was in this fight. They both took a seat in a pair of leather armchairs.

"Good. Now that we can be civil, I will humour you. Consider it an early Christmas present. I will start simply. I don't know where Ms Drummond is."

Brett was about to yell that he didn't believe her, but she raised a finger to silence him.

"And neither does Terhoff. She is looking for her, however. And I feel through our connection that she believes she is getting close. I will not deny her this search. It would be truly monstrous to deny a child vengeance for the death of her lover. Even if that lover staked himself by joining a death cult. What she does is her own business, however. And I will not aid her idiocy."

Brett didn't reply. He couldn't. His mind was a quagmire. Overwhelmed by many things, but one above all. The vampires didn't have Kat. And that meant he had been chasing windmills while she was somewhere else entirely. His rage at Kruger abated swiftly. Not his roiling hatred for vampire-kind, but his immediate anger at a monster who had wronged him. Kruger didn't have Kat. And she didn't know what had happened to Kat. That meant Brett had been wasting time. Guilt replaced rage and he wanted to heave.

"I hear carolling," Kruger said. "My men are returning. Don't worry. I'll tell them to let you pass. You are lucky that you didn't kill any of my own in your fruitless crusade. If anything, you only removed some bad apples from my extended flock."

The chairs underneath Brett and Guy disappeared, and they found themselves standing, being unconsciously ushered out. They passed pale men wearing black business suits and tuxes, who smiled at each other with fanged grins and glared at them with red eyes.

The front gates to the estate opened for them and closed, leaving them on the empty street.

Finally, they felt lucid again, but what had happened was too real to have been a dream.

Guy fell to his knees.

"We...we didn't kill her," he lamented. "I have failed. My family. My...everything."

"I don't think we could ever kill her," Brett said, realising something for the first time in his life. Something that brought him heartache, but also a sense of sombre understanding. "She isn't the head of the snake. She's a hydra. You cut-off one head, and another hundred takes its place. Maybe…maybe, she is an evil we must accept."

Brett offered his friend a hand. Guy considered it, and then grabbed on, lifting himself up. They walked through the Constantia streets. Their mission failed, but they now realised it could never truly be won.

Chapter 14. Presents

Lost to the darkness.

That's what Treth had said. We didn't chat often after that. I felt his presence. Always there. Always watching. I felt his honest concern. And that, in his own way, he loved me. That he still cared about me. That the reason for his anger was because he cared about me. And that I was putting myself in danger. He no longer trusted that I knew what I was doing.

I didn't trust myself, to be honest.

My hunter brain told me to run. To go in for the kill. To flee or fight. But I didn't. I embraced my prey. And, I couldn't help but not only pity her, but to love her in my own peculiar way.

I didn't allow myself to fall into idleness as I did before. I insisted that Candace set up a gym for me. She did within a few hours. Dumbbells, treadmill, rowing machine, punching bags...the works. I got back into shape. Earned my showers. It didn't feel as good as chopping up undead (Candace didn't seem to like that idea), but at least I was working up a sweat.

Candace and I had an odd relationship. Even if one ignored our professions. I acted like a big sister, yet she bought me everything I asked for. Like a sugar-mommy. She doted on me materially. As if bribing me to stay. To be honest, the gifts made the stay almost bearable, but they were not what kept me there. All I really wanted was to leave. I missed my cat and my pixie. I missed my friends. Hell, I even missed Conrad Khoi. And Brett…

I wondered what Treth would think of Brett now that Team Colin was no longer relevant. The darkness of the humour gave me a quick, dry chuckle before it made me want to gag. Yet, I found myself thinking about Brett quite a lot. I hoped he was okay. What was he up to? He could be pretty gung-ho. I hoped he didn't do anything stupid. The guy annoyed the hell out of me sometimes, but he was sweet.

Before it was all over, I hoped to see him again.

And that brought me to the key issue:

When it was all over.

When I was released. When Candace either overcame the darkness or was consumed by it. When she failed to bring back her parents, or somehow succeeded. And my entire world would be destroyed.

Treth didn't understand. He took it as a given that Candace would fail. That she was lost, and I was on the verge of becoming a necromancer apprentice, if I wasn't already.

I was angry at first, but I soon realised what was going through his head. He had watched his brother consumed by the darkness. The same brother who had murdered the love of his life and then him. To see me, his home and (I would think) best friend play with a necromancer…it must have been heart breaking.

I tried to reason with him, keeping all this in mind. But even if I could be thoughtful and empathetic on occasion, I was still Kat Drummond. And Kat Drummond doesn't mince words and struggles with drama.

"She can't be saved," Treth bluntly put, when we argued over my decision to stay.

"But I must try. I know what happened to you…"

"You don't know a thing!" he yelled.

And I lost it. "I will save her, Treth! I'll show you."

Because if I couldn't save her, could I truly save myself?

***

It was Christmas day and I had made a card for Candace using some scrap and stationary I found around the stronghold. A simple A5 piece of white cardboard with some string glued down in the shape of a reindeer, with some red shiny paper stuck over the nose to make it into Rudolph. I enjoyed making it. I think the last time I made something like it was before my parents died.

I put the finishing touches on the card the morning of Christmas day, ending it off with a simple "Merry Christmas" message. Treth considered the card, with a hint of distaste and anxiety. We weren't speaking at the moment. He was being a right fool. Yet, I was also sad even as I smiled at my handiwork. It would be the first Christmas in years away from Trudie's family. Normally, I would help her mom set up the table for Christmas lunch, and then we would unwrap presents. Trudie's family weren't rich, but they always made sure to get me something. To include me as a member of the family.

I didn't really understand until recently that they had been my family. And that Trudie was not just my best friend, but my sister.

And by Athena, I was going to kill her boyfriend.

The thought disturbed me but did not deter me. Andy would die. Painfully, if I could help it. I would deal with the fallout afterwards. That is, assuming that Trudie didn't see what he did to Colin. If she had, then she would be on my side. She could be a bit of an airhead occasionally, but she wasn't a fool.

Candace wasn't home. Yet, unlike before, she had told me her plans. She had some reagents to gather. Errands to run. Everything was coming to fruition. And, she needed to pick up something for Christmas. She told me to expect her back just before dinner.

After making her card, I spent an hour in the gym. Treth sulked in his corner, but I felt him judging my boxing form. Or was that admiration? I had a connection with Treth, but reading his emotions was more an art than a science. And emotions can be complicated.

After my gym session, I showered and got into some jeans and a black t-shirt that Candace had acquired for me. I really felt like a dependent. I wasn't used to it. But I had to be. Not like I could or should pay rent to my complex captor. I just had to grit my teeth and accept the gifts. It's not like they were actually bribes. I had decided not to kill Candace already. Yet, at least. Some clothes and weights weren't going to change my mind either way.

I was much more pathetic than that, my nasty inner voice said. All Candace had to do was cry, and I'd cave.

How would I kill a crying wight? All a vampire would need to do now is pout and I'd put down my swords and give it a hug. Pfft. I would need to re-train after all this. To get hard again. A soft monster hunter was a dead monster hunter.

The dining room was closed off with a message from Candace telling me to only go in after 7PM. I stuck to the lounge and kitchen area, made myself a simple lunch of instant noodles (very festive) and read some comics and books. Finally, the clock showed 7PM, and I made my way to the dining room.

I was greeted by a roaring fire, despite the summer heat, a traditional Christmas music record, and an almost fully decorated Christmas tree, with Candace standing on a foot-stool, trying to put the star on top. She almost toppled as I entered.

"You're early!"

"I'm right on time."

Candace pouted. "I'm not finished yet."

Her pout turned to a grin. "You can put the star on top."

I considered the tall tree. It was almost double the height of the tree that Trudie's family got every year.

"Nah, I think you should. But, I'll help."

I offered Candace my back and let her climb on top of my shoulders. It was a strain, but I'd held off worse. The mimic's jaws were much worse. Candace placed the star on top and I feigned falling. She held on, and then laughed as I steadied and lowered her down.

After Candace had regained her footing, I searched the room. Dinner was served on the dining room table. A roast chicken dinner. Potatoes, veggies. The entire ensemble. Candace must have spent all day preparing this! Or paid someone to set it up for her. Well, I at least hope she paid someone. Slavery was not my favourite and undead slaves were definitely not my cup of tea either.

"It's the first time I've cooked a roast," Candace said, answering the question of the origins of the meal.

"I didn't see you in the kitchen today at all."

"I used the bottom floor kitchen."

"There's a bottom floor?"

Candace waved away the comment.

"It's boring. And it's where I'm keeping the zombies, so you don't have to see them."

I grimaced. Candace laughed.

"Don't worry. I kept them far away from the food. They're locked up in the garages."

My silence was answer enough and Candace frowned.

"I have to keep them somewhere."

"Why do you have to keep them at all?" I answered, keeping my voice measured, but barely hiding my distaste.

She waved away the question. "None of that will matter. Soon. Well, I think, soon. It's almost ready. And then…"

I saw the mad glint in her eye and decided to distract her.

"Here," I said, passing her the card I made.

She accepted it and examined it for what seemed a good long minute. I couldn't see her eyes and waited patiently for her reaction. I was shocked as she looked up, her eyes glistening with tears. She ambushed me with a hug, engulfing my midriff. Both Treth and I were equally surprised.

"Thank you," she whispered, her head nestled into my chest. "Thank you."

Accepting the reaction, I hugged back and patted her head. Treth registered his displeasure but didn't comment.

I didn't know if he had forgotten his humanity or if I was a fool.

Eventually, Candace let go and took a step back, tears still apparent on her cheeks.

"Anyway…" She wiped away some tears. "Let's eat."

The chicken was overcooked. The roast vegetables were undercooked. The potatoes were fine, if a bit overly salty. I loved it, and made sure to tell Candace, who insisted that it wasn't great but beamed at the compliment. It was definitely better than anything I could produce. I was not culinarily-inclined.

Upon finishing the meal, Candace promptly revealed a Christmas cake. The type covered in brandy and lit on fire.

"That smells like a distillery!" I commented.

"It's fine," she insisted, while fiddling with a lighter. I could see she was not a smoker like Trudie. Didn't know how to handle the gadget.

"No, it is not! You're 15. I didn't drink until I was 18."

She looked up, pouting. "It's Christmas."

I put my hands on my waist, attempting to look as strict as possible, but she was right. It was Christmas. And now that I thought about it, Trudie's mom often overpoured brandy onto the Christmas cake.

I sighed, and Candace grinned. I took the lighter from her and lit it myself. I don't smoke but being around Trudie taught me some things.

The cake was sweet and soaked in booze. I started to regret my decision to let Candace have it. A drunk 15-year-old girl was one thing, but a drunk 15-year-old necromancer was another. As I ate each bite, I became giddier. I could also see Candace getting heady, but she looked like she was enjoying herself.

The cake was finally finished. I'm sure it was meant for four people, but we polished it off ourselves.

"Presents!" Candace suddenly cried out and bolted to the tree.

I made my way there more methodically, even as this girl buzzed with excitement. Besides her bouts of intellectualism and her definitely adult-like propensity for dark magic, Candace really acted a lot younger than her years. Perhaps, it was to compensate for having to grow up too fast in other ways. I definitely grew up too fast. Missed out on a lot.

Below the Christmas tree were three parcels. Two were long and one was massively large. They all had my name on them.

My card felt very inadequate right now.

"Open them," Candace insisted, nodding like a child. She didn't seem to mind the inequality.

I bent down and sat on my knees. The largest parcel was before me and I reached out for it. I felt a tingling sensation as I touched the wrapping but didn't pull back my hand. It felt...alive. But familiar. I felt a throbbing. Almost at the back of my head. Treth felt it too.

I tore open a sliver in the wrapping and almost wept. It was my coat. My wonderful coat. In all its orange and scaly glory. I had missed it. But it wasn't just the coat as I left it, cooling and dry. As I touched it, it flared up, enveloping the wrapping in flames that did not burn me. Candace didn't seem shocked as the Christmas wrapping turned to cinders. She probably knew more about it than I.

"How?" I asked, in a whisper. Last time I had worn the coat, I had pushed it too hard. I thought it had died.

"Death is never the end. But your coat wasn't even dead." She shrugged, adopting her more scholarly persona. "Salamanders, when in great stress, hibernate. All I had to do was feed it a bit of healing magic and it awoke."

The coat glowed in my hands.

"It likes you," she said.

"I killed it."

"It doesn't have any hard feelings, then."

I stood and put it on. Flames erupted around me as I pirouetted. It felt so good to be on my back again. It hummed, and I knew it felt the same way.

"There's more," Candace said, handing me one of the longer parcels.

I opened it without hesitation but stopped. The worn hand-guard of my dusack. That meant the other parcel contained my wakizashi. I looked up at Candace.

"Why?"

"It was easy," she said, ignoring the question. "No security at your apartment. Not anymore. I snuck in and got them myself."

"What about my cat? And Duer?"

"Both are living with your friend."

"Trudie?"

"No. The woman with the Holy Light vestment and the sad eyes."

"Cindy?" That would make sense. Trudie loved Alex, but her family didn't like cats. I was glad that Duer and Alex had a home. And maybe through their ordeal of moving, they would find some common ground and stop going at each other's throats.

Candace nodded.

"But that still doesn't answer my question. Why arm me? I could just as easily use this against you."

"I trust you, Kat," she said, straight-faced and as adult-like as I had ever seen her. "And more than that, I need you to be you. It's because I'm a failure, and you represent how I have failed. Your bravery. Your skill. Your ability to just keep on going. You are a warrior. And I have needed to be a warrior in the past but have failed. I am a mage, for better or worse. But every mage needs a warrior. A swordsman…or swordswoman."

"You had Marshal," I said. "He was your sword."

"Marshal was tired." There was an unmistakable hint of sadness in her voice, and a look of listlessness in her eyes. "The only reason I agreed to your duel was that I knew he wanted to die. I could not deny him his end."

There was silence, as I couldn't reply. In the silence, I felt Treth's curiosity, and an unmistakable melancholy.

Did he want to die, and was I keeping him from his promised end?

Candace broke the silence and the reverie.

"It should be about time."

"Time for what?"

"The Christmas lights."

Candace stood and led me to the fireplace. She whispered a word and the fire died. Another word, and the fireplace opened up into a doorway, leading into a stairwell. We ascended the stairs. Higher and higher, until we opened up onto the roof I had stood on during my escape attempt.

Despite the darkness, Table Mountain in the distance was lit up with greens, whites and reds. A Santa Claus flew across the sky, then exploded into a dragon that strafed across the blackened hull of the Titan's mountain, landing and becoming a forest filled with reindeer.

The lights shifted between telling a story, and just revelling in the splendour of what humanity could achieve with its forays into magic. It wasn't something so complex as Pranish's lawmancy, or as twisted as Candace's necromancy. It was just a light-show. Beautiful. Impractical. Utterly useless in the long run. But it brought a tear to my eye and made me think of a time before I had been so cynical.

Candace gripped my hand and I squeezed.

A peculiar couple, we were. A necromancer and an undead hunter, standing on a rooftop, watching the lights above one of the wonders of the world.

"I have another gift for you," Candace whispered, coyly, as an illusionary drake lit up her eyes. "But I'm afraid."

"Afraid of what?"

"That you'll go, this time."

"I can't stay here forever. No matter if I forgive you or not."

"I don't expect you to forgive me, Kat. I just want you to be with me. To remind me that I'm human. But I know that you have your own mission. And I must not be selfish, even though I want to be."

"What is it, Candy?"

"The werewolf. The thing that killed your love. I know where he resides. My crows have shown me."

All other thoughts ceased, and the distant flashes of magical fireworks became irritants in the corner of my eyes.

"Where?" Treth recoiled slightly at the iciness in my voice. Candace did not seem to notice.

"A villa. I have the address written down. But..."

"I have to kill him."

"I know, but…but…what if you don't come back?"

"Candy, I'm not really here. Not here. Not anywhere. I'm in a funk. A dark fog. I don't even know that it's really Christmas. And it isn't because I've been stuck here. It is because I have left something unfulfilled. I've got a vendetta. And I'm not one to let vendettas go. Treth may not trust you, but I think…I hope, that there is still real good in you. I want to save you. I truly do. But if I am to save you, I need to save myself. And that means killing that monster."

"I know," she said again, with a bit of a choked sob. "But out there…there're people who want to take you away. And even if you want to come back, you won't be able to. They won't let me have you. And without you, I don't think I'll stave off the madness long enough to even be able to bring my parents or you back. But if you don't go, then I still can't complete my purpose."

"What do you mean?"

"The final ingredient I need is the blood of a werewolf, taken by one with a hate-filled heart."

She laughed, but she didn't sound amused.

"Fate is a fickle bitch. It's as if she was plotting this the entire time. She makes me risk you, of all people. For I know my other servants couldn't do this. They don't hate anyone. They can't. But you…No! I cannot. We cannot. I won't let you die and, without you, the madness may drive me to do something I will truly regret, despite the coldness the darkness makes me feel."

A thought struck me. I didn't know why I thought about it, or how, but it was a way to solve all of this.

"What if there was a way that I could leave this place and get my revenge, without leaving you?"

"Hmmm?"

I indicated for her to go inside. It was getting windy. "I've got an idea," I said.

She nodded and entered. I entered after her but stopped long enough to stare into the eyes of a colossal white wolf, perched on Table Mountain, illusionary lights spiralling around its paws. It stared back at me.

"I'm coming for you," I whispered. "No matter the cost."

Chapter 15. Fate

"You know how many years you have been my student?" the Mentor asked, his voice calm, but I shuddered all the same. I had failed him again. Failed my master. My mentor. The one who would help me bring back all that was dear to me. The one who helped me through the pain in my head.

"I…I…"

He held up his finger to shush my stuttering. His expression was impassive, but I could sense his disappointment, rising like a burning stench off a trash-fire. All my cumulative failures were piling up. Festering.

"It has been four years. And you are yet to properly control the undead. Your mastery of flesh puppetry is impressive, but no necromancer can rely on puppets alone. Necromancers need zombies. The risen dead. And more than that, they need the dead to OBEY."

The last word approximated a shout but didn't quite approach that volume. I almost flinched. Almost.

He sighed and turned away.

"How do you expect to bring back your loved ones if you can't even stop your own risen from attacking you? It is expected for any student of the Graffscripp to struggle with their control, initially. You raised your first corpse in record time. I didn't care that it was rogue then. Because my first zombie also went rogue. And so did my master's. It is to be expected. We had not fully embraced the darkness. Had not truly known the full extent of what it could do for us. What we should do for it. We feared it. And I can see, even now, that you still fear it. You seek to chain it up and use it like an enraged hound. But that isn't how to treat our shared power. The dark arts are worthy of respect, and only those virtuous enough to realise themselves unworthy of its power, truly deserve to use it."

I looked down at my toes. Barefoot. On cold, white tiles. Dried blood in the cracks. My shame brought the pain back three-fold, but I didn't show it. I was becoming used to it.

I felt a hand on my shoulder and looked up. The Mentor's concerned eyes sent a warm pang through my heart.

"Candace, my dear Candace. The pain can and will stop. You only need to give in. To accept the darkness. To let it serve you by you serving it. This isn't something that you can negotiate. You will only find pain and madness if you persist down this path of contradiction. Accept all of it, or none of it."

He stood up straight and smiled.

"I know, that in the end, you will make the right choice."

I wasn't so certain. He left, but I found myself standing in the cold ritual room, a beheaded zombie crumpled in the corner. Another physical testament to my failure. It had lunged for Mentor. Lunged at my master! He had every reason to be angry at me. In fact, it would be good if he shouted at me. I deserved to be chastised for failing him all these years. When he had been so kind. As he had helped me grow to this point.

But I was growing no longer.

I rushed through the double doors towards the freezer room of Mentor's Hope City stronghold, holding back my tears. I couldn't cry. Not now. Not when my mom and dad weren't there to comfort me. To stop my crying. I had to be strong.

I rubbed the threat of tears from my eyes as I arrived at a freezer door. I unlatched it and slid it open. The room was filled with rows and rows of body-bags, kept crisp by intensive cooling. Dominating the centre were two bags, held by hooks, side-by-side. The tops of the bags were open, revealing the faces of my parents. Both did not maintain the features I remembered in their final moments. No screaming. No crying. No blood-stained chin and cheeks. I had seen to it that they wouldn't. They needed to be clean. Pristine. The parents I would bring back. Not the dead parents I would never see again.

"Hi mom. Hi dad," I said.

As usual, they did not reply.

I sighed and took a seat on the concrete floor, cross-legged.

"I don't know what I'm supposed to do. Mentor keeps telling me everything that I must do. And I try to do it…I really do. But…some of it feels wrong. But how can it be wrong? He is trying to help me. He is the only one who has. Who can. But I keep disobeying him."

I stared at their faces, fixedly. Eyes closed. As if they were asleep. Yet their skin was pale and icy. I looked at my lap. My feet were cold. I should have put shoes on.

"I can't give in to the darkness. I know he tells me to, but something holds me back. I think…I think…it's you. Because I can't give up on you and accepting the darkness means giving up on everything else. But if I give up on you, then what was the point?"

I spoke the last few words at a rapid pace, and stopped to take some hurried breaths, before collapsing onto the floor to stare at the blank ceiling and listen to the vibrations of the cooling system.

"Would you know what to do, dad? Did you know what you were doing? Do I know what I'm doing?"

A tear did escape my eye.

"Can I really bring you back?"

I left the freezer and even the slightly warmer air of the lab was not enough to thaw the chill on my bare skin. I made my way to the dining room. If the fire wasn't lit, I would light it myself. I had learnt some basic pyromancy. Might as well. Needed to be good at something. At least the fire didn't need to obey me. It just needed to burn.

The fire was already lit in the dining room and Mentor was sitting in his armchair, reading. I approached, softly, so not to disturb him. There was no music playing and the record player was skipping, creating a methodical and static thumping. The back of the Mentor's head was steady, and I stopped to admire his black hair. It seemed to always maintain its length and style. Unchanging. Undying. It added to why he was such a great master. He was a certainty. Any failure, I realised, was mine as the student. I would need to take his lessons seriously. But, how could I? Perhaps, I should talk with him about it.

I seldom spoke to the Mentor about my feelings. I didn't want to bore him. It wasn't my place to lay my petulant angst on him. But, if my fears could be allayed, and I could finally move on...then it was worth embarrassing myself.

My decision made, I approached him. I was about to speak when what the Mentor was holding stopped me. He wasn't reading a book, a scroll or a tome, but was rather staring at a colour photograph. His expression was one of warmth and curiosity. The type of face he made when he reassured me that my failures were not the end. That I could be a great necromancer. I just had to try harder. To prove him right. And that I would prove him right. Because he was never wrong.

"Master..." I murmured.

The Mentor didn't stop looking at the photo as he spoke.

"Time doesn't seem constant, does it?"

"Time, master?"

"Four years, I have had you. Yet, it seems longer. Like time has drawn farther and farther way. But…" he gripped the edge of the photograph tighter. "Ten years seems frightfully short. As if my mind right now only really considered my youth real, and that everything now is just a dream of routine."

He sighed.

"Master, who is the girl?"

The girl with dark chestnut hair and blue eyes, holding an ice cream at the park, flanked by two smiling parents.

"When I was younger," he replied. "I was more ambitious. I wanted to understand this world. To tame it. To dominate it. In more recent years, I've realised that I cannot. And that more can be accomplished by being subservient to the elements than trying to enslave them. Even so, I am still proud of what I accomplished in my formative years."

He traced a finger over the picture of the girl.

"I wanted to know if I could create a storage mechanism for demons and spirits. A Vessel, if you will. To have a focus for the incorporeal and beings of the In Between would have helped me more effectively with my adjustments of the undead. And…I simply wanted to see if I could do it."

He smiled, and promptly frowned.

"I think I succeeded. The girl absorbed the souls effectively during testing, but before I could trap them, I was…interrupted. Puretide, the meddlers that they are, forced me to flee."

A warm smile returned to his lips.

"But she is still out there. And doing well, if my birds see correctly. She has a heart full of hate. Some think her soul broken by what she has gone through. But I know better. It isn't broken. She just has many of them. Many souls. Sharing one body. Imagine it, Candace?"

I didn't reply. I stared at the picture of the smiling girl. She was about the age I was when my parents were killed.

"She is amazing, isn't she?" he said, and I recognised the tone in his voice. Pride. The same prideful voice he spoke in when I did something right. The voice that vindicated his love for me.

But he spoke in the same way about a picture. Of a girl with many souls. And a subtle voice in my head told me: "He is proud of himself. He doesn't really care about you."

"But he protects me," I wanted to reply.

"Because he doesn't want his things to break."

His *things*.

I left the room. The Mentor didn't notice my leaving. In my quarters, I didn't cry. I only discerned an almost alien feeling grow and boil inside my stomach. Anger. No, rage…. No… Hate. Betrayal. Treachery!

I wasn't a thing. And I wouldn't be a thing. I wouldn't accept the darkness if it would make me its thing. I would show him. I would show all of them. I wasn't a pet project. I wasn't just some photo to sneer at. I was a modern Prometheus. And I'd sooner watch the world be destroyed than just be an idle curiosity of a single man.

Chapter 16. Revenge

"Take my eye," I said, without hesitation as I lay down on the cold-metal surgical table dominating the centre of the lab.

"What?!" Treth screamed.

"It's simple," I explained out loud to Candace, more for Treth's benefit than hers'. "Take my eye and give me yours. It will allow you to create a vision-link. You will feel my presence and see what I see. If me being near keeps the madness at bay, then this should more than hold it back. It also means you can see that I'm okay."

Candace considered me, pulling and rubbing the cuffs of her black hoodie. She breathed rapidly. Anxiously.

Treth continued to wail at me. "You've been mindwarped. Break out of it! This isn't you, Kat. We kill necromancers. We don't swap eyes with them."

"Shut up, Treth!" I yelled, and then looked at Candace. My gaze was not meant to be intimidating, but the intensity of it caused Candace to take a step back.

"I need to do this, Candace. And if letting you cut my eye out is what it will take, then I'll do it. I don't fucking care about some vendetta against necromancy anymore. At least, not for now. I have to kill him. And if making a deal with the darkness is what it takes, I'll do it."

"It's not worth it," Treth whispered. I felt his tears fall on my lap. I looked up and caught a flash of his visage, as I had seen him months before when the archdemon came a handspan away from killing me. He was so young. The age I was when we had met. But I had aged, and he had not. And I had grown enough to know that one had to make sacrifices.

"You would have made a powerful necromancer," Candace said, the scholarly tone dominating her voice, but I could hear trepidation. "Far more powerful than I. You understand what swapping our eyes will do?"

"You will see what I see."

She nodded. "Mainly. But you may also see what I see. Glimpses of my psyche. And I must warn you, Kat…my friend…what I see is not something you can just shrug off. I am broken and, by trying to pick me up, you will risk cutting yourself on broken glass."

"I am already damaged. Perhaps not in the same way as you are, but I have faced death so many times. It has scarred me. So much. But every time…every time…"

My breath caught in my throat, and I felt Treth look at me. Despair. Defeat. Love. He didn't understand. Didn't understand what I had gone through. And what I needed to do.

"I got up," I finished. "And I killed it. Whatever it was. And I killed the next thing. And the next. And every time I didn't die, I broke into more and more pieces. I don't know what you've seen, Candace, but I've seen my own horrors. And if I have to see yours as well, I will just get back up again."

She leaned on the counter, to balance herself. I had never seen her this nervous before. It wasn't like her childlike fright, or her bouts of paranoid madness. This was the intelligent Candace. The one who had to grow up too fast. And she was frightened.

"Eye or not, it is dangerous. He's not just a werewolf, you know? He's an alpha. With a pack."

"More dangerous than a vampire god or an arch-necromancer?"

She paused. "I guess not...but you had help, both times."

"You can help me."

The thought of fighting alongside the undead sickened me, but if it meant putting Andy in the ground…

She shook her head.

"I cannot. My empire is crumbled."

"What? I thought you were the Necrolord. You owned what seemed to be half the slums."

"Not even close," she said. "And now I own only this stronghold. And it isn't even mine. I hold it as long as my Mentor remains missing. I am not sure I could keep him out if he ever returned."

"But…but what happened to your flesh factories? Your other strongholds? Your abominations and armies?"

"Down to just a few," she said, and smiled, weakly. "Without the Marshal, I couldn't do anything else. And with you, I regained some of my lost conscience. It didn't feel right, anymore, to do what I was doing."

"For Athena's sake! You're a necromancer."

"And you hate necromancers, Kat. And I didn't want to upset you anymore. I stopped making new minions only a week after you arrived. And it has hurt. The darkness and madness both tell me that I need more. More minions. More and more…"

She stopped as the voice of madness came to her. She took a deep breath, and her lucidity returned.

"I didn't need my empire anymore. After you arrived, I realised that. I just needed you. To complete the balance. To hold back the madness. To show me the power of light."

"But if you don't get your final ingredient, you won't be able to bring back your parents," I said.

"Do you believe I can? That it is possible that I will see them again?"

Did I? I felt Treth's doubt. He was sure it would fail. He was so confident that it would that he gave no thought to if he wanted it to succeed or not. But, what did I feel?

It violated all the rules. Necromancy didn't return life. It controlled the dead. But rules were often broken. Candace was a testament to that. A little girl forged in darkness. Returned to the light. And constantly flickering between incompatible magic. And what about Treth? A spirit, or something else, linked to me from realms away, and bound by shared suffering.

We broke the rules.

So, who was I to doubt Candace?

But it was more than that. I wanted Candace to be right. I wanted her to see her parents again. To be happy. To have the chance I did not have at being a little girl again.

But more than that, I wanted her to be wrong. For if she was right, and if she did bring back her parents, and they were living and capable of a truly human happiness with their daughter, then it meant that I picked the wrong side. And that I could have seen my parents again. That I could have brought them back.

"I don't know," I answered, finally.

Candace nodded. And seemed to regain her composure and confidence.

"Are you sure about this?"

"Yes," I replied, and really meant it.

"You will still be able to see out of my eye in your socket but may catch glimpses of what your eye sees in mine."

"I know."

"You must reach out to your allies when outside," she said.

Brett.

"I will."

I heard Treth whimper, but he didn't yell. He retreated to his chamber.

I lay down on the table and closed my eyes. I felt the warmth of the miasma roll over me and smelled the distinct smell of roses, even as my consciousness faded away.

Chapter 17.Conclave

The Mentor met with many people, but never at his own safehouses and strongholds. Always at another location. Away from me. I used to not think about this. It was like any parent leaving for work. A child didn't constantly ponder the reason their parent left for work every day. But since growing colder towards the Mentor, I started to realise why he didn't bring his colleagues to me. I was not ready. One did not show off an incomplete project. They kept it hidden. At least, until it had a new layer of paint and glitz. Until it was presentable. In the past, I had not been presentable.

But not this time.

The Mentor told me that his colleagues were coming over for an important meeting and a group of men and women promptly arrived at the stronghold, wearing black formalwear. A few greeted me as I quietly looked on. They were varying ages. Not all had the look of mages. Some had the insincere smiles of a showman or politician. Others seemed more genuinely pleasant and asked me about my hobbies. I couldn't tell them much. Learning under the Mentor was my hobby. One I was almost flagging at. And while I previously thought the Mentor patient, I could now see through his tempered responses. He was sick of waiting. I was a failing project, only good enough to impress the brief glances of some colleagues as they passed through the halls. How long would he give me until he moved on?

I had to do better. Not for him. Not anymore. But to ensure I could use him. I needed him. And that meant I had to keep going. As his toy, or not.

Usually, I'd be churning through Graffscripp or practicing my casting, but today I was expected to stand at the entrance of the stronghold, allowing the Mentor's colleagues to gawk at his curiosity. A little girl he had trained into some semblance of a necromancer. For most of the guests, it seemed that the black robe, too large for my frame, was impressive enough. They smiled my way and then continued into the conference room. If only they knew that while I could make the dead rise, I could not make them do my bidding?

I held my hands behind my back, fidgeting with the fabric of my robe as more people passed. One stopped to talk to the Mentor, who was standing by my side, shaking hands with his colleagues as they entered his home.

"I would love to see a demonstration, Monsieur White," a tubby man with a certain sliminess to him announced, interrupting a handshake between the Mentor and a woman wearing a pearl necklace. I recognised the tubby man. From newspapers. I knew by his accent and his name that he was not really French.

"Minister," the Mentor replied, baring his teeth in a smile that only I could tell was forced. "So glad that you could make it."

"I have always envied your art, White. And to teach it to a child? Stupendous! A demonstration. Please."

The Mentor looked at me. Both our expressions were impassive. He looked back at the minister.

"We do not really have any corpses on hand…"

The Mentor stopped as the minister revealed the corpse of a dead pigeon, secreted in his inner jacket pocket. I resisted raising an eyebrow. The minister dropped the mangled bird onto the ground, at my feet. His smile was toothy, and his teeth were too white to be real.

The Mentor eyed me. I didn't know if it was encouragement or shame. His expression was blank.

I stared at the deceased bird, wondering how it came to be like this. And how I came to be like this. Staring at a bird, in a dark room full of strangers, fearing that if I raised this bird from the dead, it would attack the minister, or the Mentor, or me. I could always puppet it, but that wasn't true reanimation and may only delay his inevitable requests for a true zombie bird.

A man with pointed ears stepped between the minister and me. He was the only man not wearing black, rather opting for an ash blue suit.

"Mr DuToit! Fancy seeing you in a place like this."

"Elf," the minister, Mr DuToit, replied, curtly. He had no humour in his voice anymore.

"Yes. Very perceptive of you."

The elf turned his head, revealing his profile. Beyond his black gelled mane of hair, he had the features I expected of an elf. Sharp angles. A longish nose. And piercing purple eyes. He smiled, and I couldn't help but feel uncomfortable. His expression explained more than words ever could about this man. There was no hint of insecurity. No question about his own capacity, power or goals. Only confidence. Not arrogance. Arrogance was misplaced. The truly self-assured could not be arrogant. This man had full knowledge of his power, and nobody had ever successfully said "no" to him before.

"Zieg, let us leave our generous host and ward for now. I have things to discuss."

Reluctantly, the minister allowed himself to be dragged away by the elf. When they had entered the conference room, the Mentor looked at me pointedly.

"To your room. And no leaving until I come for you. That clear?"

His tone shocked me. The Mentor had never truly been strict with me before. And had never resorted to this commanding tone in the past.

"Yes, master," I said. He nodded and entered after his guests.

I considered the dead pigeon on the floor and picked it up.

On the way to my room, I couldn't get the image of the elf out of my head. He was too intense to be attractive. At least, too alien for me to find him attractive. But he had an aura that allowed for no disobedience. Even though the minister was curt with him, he still obeyed, following the elf like a well-trained puppy. That sort of authority was not something I had encountered before in my studies. My work concerned the darkness. How to use it. How to serve it. The technical aspects of its usage and its nature. And I had come to believe that the darkness was the crucial aspect to my work. And in a way, it was. Without it, the dead wouldn't rise. I would not be any closer to bringing back my parents. But I had not mastered the darkness. Nor did I succumb to it as the master wished. I could not. So, I played a game of grasping at a fire, but stopping short just before getting burned. And while I felt the heat, I truly did not understand the fire.

The fire was the darkness. The darkness was my vocation. My method. My master. But...but...not my servant. And that was how it was meant to be, the master said. But I considered the elf. The way he walked like the floor was his domain, and everything else was mere pawns. He did not serve anyone.

And I realised what I had not understood.

I placed the dead pigeon on my bed and recalled the words I had memorised over and over. The echoes of past headaches came back to me and I willed them away.

First, I incanted the rites of reanimation, imbuing the dead flesh of my avian quarry with the veneer of true vitality. It twitched and its little chest and wings throbbed. Without pausing, I moved onto the incantation of control. The words I had studiously revised for years but had always failed. Because the words were only half the challenge. And it was the bargaining I had always failed at. Because I had never offered enough, I had believed. But not anymore.

"Darkness," I said. "No more games. You're mine."

My words stopped and the corpse of the pigeon stopped twitching and rose.

I moved towards my pillow, in case it became necessary to smother the rogue zombie pigeon. The bird only stood up, its mangled feet straightening. It was only recently dead, and if not for its blank and unnatural stare, could have been a living bird.

I considered the creature on my bed and reached out my hand. It did not move. No hint of hunger or rage. Just an undead bird, standing like a statue.

I sent forth my will, and it flew up to my hand, where it perched.

My heart skipped a beat, even as a grin lit up my face. It took everything in me not to scream with joy. I would need to show the Mentor. Show him that he wasn't wrong. That I wasn't a failure!

No...

I was not his thing. Not his project.

But if he knew I had made progress, then it would bring me closer to bringing them back.

I couldn't wait for the Mentor to be done with his meeting, however. I needed to see what I could do. To make up for the time I had lost, not using my powers as a master rather than a servant.

I incanted a short phrase, touching the eyeball of the pigeon, and then the mirror in my room. My reflection disappeared and was replaced with the image of a much larger me from another angle. I willed the bird to fly and, as it did so, the image on my mirror changed angles dramatically and I shrank. The pigeon circled and the footage in the mirror revolved around my image.

I beamed. Never had I progressed far enough for a necromantic sensory-link to be possible. But my room was too small for it to be truly a test of my powers. I needed my bird to soar. To explore. To be my eyes where I could not go.

A thought occurred to me and I willed the bird to rise towards the grate on the ceiling. The cracks between the bars were just large enough for it to pass through.

A sensation of rushing air and the thumping of the ventilation caught me off-guard. While the mirror transmitted the bird's vision, I hadn't anticipated that I would feel its other sensations and hear what it heard.

It was better than I could imagine. I sent the bird flying. Felt the rush of air on my flesh. Heard the wind in my ears. I closed my own eyes and became one with the creature I had risen. And in that act, I flew. Through the maze of shafts in this stronghold. Up bends, around corners. More dextrous than any real bird. As if the faculties of both the bird in life and my own skill had been combined to create something better.

I lost track of time and all my actual sensations were replaced by that of my bird. And in the tunnels, I found myself becoming lost, but not caring. For I had no troubles here. Just the air. Just flight.

I fell to my knees as I felt a spike of pain in my head and I had to stop to catch my breath. I had pushed myself. Too far. Too fast. I still felt the bird, on the periphery of my consciousness, but we were no longer one.

"Come on, Candace. Have some sense," I told myself, out-loud. I sent my perception back into the bird, but not as strongly. I needed to be an observer. Not the bird itself.

The bird had landed in the shaft and seemed unhurt. Not that the undead could be hurt easily. I prepared it to fly again, when I heard muffled voices.

The Mentor's meeting. A naughty thought came to me, and I sent my bird towards the sound of the voices.

"The Shadow War is over," a voice of one of the guests stated, simply. I stopped my bird and listened.

"It never really started. It can't really end. You're acting as if we have completed our goals," responded another.

"The League is dead! The Empire is captured. The Magocracy has been ours for decades."

"Yet, Hope City still eludes us."

"Eludes us?" the voice of Minister DuToit came. "Half of the cabinet sit here. We own Hope City! More than the Conclave owns the Empire. At least we are not mere puppets, like the Zulu Emperor."

"Puppets obey," the elf replied, his voice smooth, yet menacing.

"Puppets can cut their strings." That input by the Mentor silenced them both. He continued.

"Hope City is bound by the Spirit of the Law. We could capture every single position on the Council, and it wouldn't change a thing. What is required is a breakdown in the weylines of the city."

"Which would make the city useless."

"Correct, Mr Garce, but the breakdown need not be permanent. It must only be long enough to allow us to seize power. To prevent the weylines powering the Spirit of the Law."

"So, I see two steps to this. First, the breakdown of the weylines. Second, securing the seat of the city in time," the elf added.

"Correct. As it stands, our goals remain unchanged. The League and its destruction were never our primary goal. Just an obstacle. With its last vestiges gone, Dawi's pet project can remain dead. Like him."

He paused and nobody interjected.

"Ladies and gentlemen, we will not make the same mistakes as our forebears. Victorum fell because it lacked ambition. Because it tried to kill what it felt it could not control. It was ruled by fear. And in that fear, it let maniac mercenaries become its representatives. No...we won't become like them. We must not fear. Not the League. Not the agencies. No one. For our destiny is already written.

The Conclave will deliver salvation to this world. That, I am sure of."

"What about the girl?" a woman asked.

"Excuse me?" the Mentor sounded incredulous.

"The girl. Your student. The one who killed Brutus."

"Oh," the Mentor sounded like he had recalled some vague piece of knowledge. "A side project. Nothing more."

"How did you convince her to become the student of the man who called for her parents' deaths?" the woman sounded amused, just as I lost my ability to hear anything else.

I was overcome with a myriad of emotions. Rage, I recognised. Betrayal. Sadness. Despair. But also, many others, forming a quagmire I couldn't explain.

The Mentor. My master…

I couldn't believe it. But I had to. Because it made too much sense. Because I should have seen it before.

He had killed them.

But I couldn't kill him now. No matter how much I wanted to. Because he was the only key I had to bringing them back. And after I was done with him, I would let my risen eat him alive.

I lived a careful balancing act in the time that followed. I acted childishly, younger than my years, in order to avoid any risk of my rage coming through to reveal my true feelings. I feigned seeking his praise like a desperate dog. When I got it, I pretended to be happy that I had made master smile. And yes, I made master smile a lot.

In the days that followed, I raised and controlled my first human zombie. And then more. I proceeded to shape my servants to my whim. Not just to imitate life, but to perfect it in death. I turned flesh and bone into weapons. To fight the Mentor, I told myself. Yet, my minions soon fell under his control.

Not to show any sign that I knew about his true nature, I just smiled and accepted his theft of my creatures. Rifts! Even so it pained me to do so. I wanted to scream. I wanted to tear his eyes out myself.

But…I was no warrior. Pathetic. Weak.

I couldn't defend them.

But I could bring them back.

My head still hurt. The madness told me it was because I needed to kill the Mentor now. But I couldn't. I needed him. And I feared it was more than that. It was the darkness wanting dominion. It wasn't content to be my servant. Perhaps, the Mentor was right. For one to use the darkness for long, one needed to become its servant. But I didn't need to use it for long. I just needed to use it long enough.

I read into the symptoms of the use of dark magic when the Mentor was away. Madness was apparently a common trait. In my lucidity, I understood that I needed to find a way to keep it at bay.

The books suggested that I needed an anchor. An object of importance. A memento. Or better yet, a person to remind me that I was human.

The Mentor introduced me to the Conclave again a year later, and to a man named Jeremiah Cox. I was told that he needed me to help him create some zombies. He spoke to me about some deranged plan to save the world. I ignored him. All that this meeting meant to me was that I was allowed to finally leave the watchful gaze of the Mentor.

I went back into the world with a head full of Graffscripp, a dagger, my clothes, and a crumpled photo in my pocket of a little girl eating ice cream with her parents. I don't know why I took it.

Jeremiah was not a good necromancer. He was too concerned with mass production of zombies than creating quality minions. In between doing my part of the Conclave's agenda, I did as I had when under the tutelage of the Mentor. I read. And in one book, I found something intriguing.

I needed a person to keep me anchored from the madness. A protector for when I went off the rails, as was inevitable. But it didn't need to be human.

I left Jeremiah in the middle of his project and disappeared. As I did so, the Mentor also disappeared. Many in the Conclave suspected we had both gone to pursue the same thing. I did not know where my once master had gone. But I had travelled to Lisbon, where I came to befriend a wight that was an exception to the rules of necromancy. I called him The Marshal.

Chapter 18.Slums

The space around my eye-socket was still tender and Treth hadn't left his chamber since I had woken up. Upon regaining consciousness on the surgery table, I felt a bit groggy, but not much else. It was as if I had awoken from a short nap. It took seeing my own blue eye in Candace's head and the reflection of her hazel eye in mine to confirm that the surgery had happened at all.

A thought occurred to me.

"How did you take your eye out?"

"The same way I took out yours. But without the miasma."

Candace answered me professionally. Stoically. There was no hint of pain or trauma in her voice, despite her literally just ripping her own eye out. I knew necromancers and corruption mages had many ways to dull pain, but there was always some residual discomfort. And by discomfort, I meant agony. And yet, Candace had done it herself. To herself.

It may be a good thing I no longer considered her an enemy. I'm not sure I could have beaten her.

"I wish I could come with you," Candace said, as I got off the surgery table and put my coat back on. It glowed a warm orange at my touch.

"That would have made this eye-swapping a bit irrelevant. But you know why you can't. I need to get my friends to help me with this. I'm not sure how they would act around the Necrolord."

She nodded.

"I have a flesh-puppet with decent muscle memory for driving. He can take you as far as the roads allow."

"Thanks, Candy."

She smiled and caught me in a hug. My coat didn't singe her.

"Come back safely. Please."

I returned the hug. "I will."

***

The flesh-puppet drove an unassuming automatic Toyota Corolla out of an underground parking garage. I chose to sit in the back. I knew it was Candace controlling the creature directly, but it still made me uncomfortable. Even if the corpse was well preserved and its only mark of undeath was its pallid skin, mostly covered by balaclava, a hood and thick jacket.

The flesh-puppet drove me away from Candace's stronghold, which I now saw to be a huge, windowless structure covered in signs warning of its imminent demolition. It looked like a giant dark grey cube, surrounded by single and double storey shanties. As far as the slums went, this area wasn't too bad. The poverty was quite visible, but the sky had glimpses of blue through the storm clouds, and I couldn't smell the decay of the weyline through the windows of the car. Was Candace's constant traversal from darkness to light influencing this part of the slum? A disturbing thought - that one girl could so profoundly affect an entire area. If it was true, it made it even more important that I saved this girl. From the darkness, and possibly from herself.

I had made such great progress already, and I couldn't believe that I was being used. Because I understood what Candace was going through. And I understood that if I could have done anything to bring back my parents, I would have tried.

But yet, I needed her to fail. Because if she did not, it meant that I was wrong, and that the darkness held the key. And I'm not sure I would be able to deny it then.

The roads narrowed as the flesh-puppet progressed towards Hope City proper. I caught glimpses of Table Mountain, but the disparate structures blocked most of the horizon. In some areas, tenements rose into the skies, but looked like they would collapse under their own weight at any moment.

I came to realise that slum streets were not built for safe driving. In fact, most of them weren't built. More often than not, a slum road was just a coincidental car-sized space between unplanned shacks, barricades, debris and flaming tires.

I watched a trash-fire as the driver stopped to wait for a convoy of trucks passing over what seemed to be one of the rare main roads. I fidgeted, and began tapping on the window, becoming increasingly anxious.

How long had it been? Were they still looking for me? Were they still alive? What had happened since I was gone? And what would they think of this.

I rubbed Candace's eye in my head and felt Candace's connection. I must admit, that knowing she could see what I saw unnerved me, but it wouldn't be forever. I only needed to put up with her voyeurism until Andy was dead and she could reverse the operation. That's what Treth didn't understand. Sure, I had a necromancer's eye in my head. But it wasn't forever.

"Treth?" I whispered aloud.

I felt his presence, but he didn't reply.

I looked out the window.

"Fine, be that way."

We travelled in silence, with only the hum of the engine and the vibrations of pot-holes and debris to fill the void. I really hoped Treth would come to his senses soon. I hated fighting with him.

The car stopped, suddenly, and I almost flew forward. A flash of an image filled half my vision. Candace was looking at a white board with her writing on it.

"Road blocked. Need to go on foot. Be safe. <3."

I steadied myself and looked out the window. It looked as if a building had collapsed over the road. Underneath its rubble were the crushed remains of a car. I looked around and didn't see any semblance of a rescue team. And then I looked up at the sky. Black. And I smelled burnt rubber. I was in a dark weyline now. One not tempered by the confusion of Candace's magic.

The thought of having to go on foot in the slums filled me with dread, but I had to remind myself of what I was.

A gods-damned monster hunter! Some stench and two-bit muggers weren't anything compared to a zombie horde and vampire cartels. I would be fine.

I said that to myself, but I struggled to believe it. The slums were a different game from undead hunting. The enemies here were humans. And while I've fought and killed my share of humans, it was not something I wanted to make a habit of. And not something I'm sure I could do again and again.

But most of all, being in the slums was like being in an alien world. I didn't know how to behave. Who to fear. What to do. Or where to go.

I gulped and exited the car. The flesh-puppet put out its hand and pointed at an alley-way between a boarded-up pharmacy and a run-down building that was almost certainly a hangout for vamp blood or fae-dust junkies.

Fae.

I got excited as I realised that just past this sea of shacks, I could see my pixie again. I closed the flesh-puppets door behind me and walked into the alley.

This area of the slums was relatively empty of people. I heard cars in the distance, but saw no people, even as I passed abandoned stalls with rotting produce. I kept my swords sheathed, but found my hands stroking their pommels. I hoped that I wouldn't need to use them. Not yet, anyway. I would be using them soon enough.

Treth was outside of his chamber, but still wasn't speaking. In the empty streets and alleys, I navigated only by glimpses of Table Mountain. It was drawing closer, and if I could make it to the border-slum, I may be able to find a university bus that could take me to campus. I should have asked Candace for money, so I could order a taxi. But in our heartfelt goodbyes, the thought didn't occur to me.

"Treth," I whispered, glancing behind me, in front of me and down every passing alley entrance. "I can guess what you're thinking about me roundabout now, but you need to understand…"

I stopped as I heard a can drop. A rat scurried away, back into its hole. I released my grip on the hilt of my sword and kept moving.

"I watched my parents die, Treth. And I am not saying that means I can do what I want, but I need you to understand why that matters."

I sighed.

"Candace is me, Treth. She's me if I had walked down the darker path. She's me if I hadn't met you. But even then, I know there's enough of me inside of her for her to change. And I need to believe that I can save her. That I can save somebody."

I felt moisture on both eyes.

"I need to know that I'm not just a killer, Treth. That what I'm doing can actually change something…"

"Duck!" Treth yelled, and I did so instantly.

The man charging at me barrelled over me and the momentum carried him straight into a concrete wall. I drew both my swords as I stood and pointed them at a group of three additional men who came crawling out of the alleys. The man who had run into the wall was not in the best of shape, but I saw what he had dropped. A crude knife. A crude and sharp knife.

"Fuck off!" I shouted, always the charmer.

"You got a pretty jacket," one of the muggers said. "You pretty underneath it?"

His friends snickered.

"I don't think you understand, boys. I'm a lieutenant of the Necrolord. If you don't go back to the shite-hole you call a home, you will have to face their wrath!"

They all laughed, even the one nursing his head injury.

"Necrolord doesn't mean shit anymore. Now take off that jacket and drop those big knives or we're gonna have to make you."

"Not scared of the Necrolord's wrath?" I asked and couldn't help but smirk. "Then face mine!"

I lashed out faster than any of them could react. My dusack met the front man's cheek, ripping a tear that made his mouth just a bit lopsided. My wakizashi found its mark in the thigh of a mugger who tried to flank me. I pulled back to assess the damage. They looked at me like I was a monster and ran. All except the man with the sore head. He reached for his knife on the ground and I kicked him in the head. He dropped. Lights out.

The alley was quiet.

"Thanks for the call-out," I said.

"I'm angry with you. Doesn't mean I want you dead," was Treth's reply.

"Love you too, Treth." He reddened.

The walk was uneventful and remained eerily quiet. But it wasn't as bad as before. Knowing I could handle the slum's particular brand of foes, I walked with a steadier step. Treth didn't speak again, but I didn't mind as much. We had been through so much more. We'd get over this.

What was a bit of necromancy-sympathising between friends?

The entanglement of alleys opened up to a street where I was greeted by the very welcome sound of hooting and road rage. It was loud. It was obnoxious. It was life, and it wasn't currently trying to kill me.

I stepped forward and took in the noise and the smells of street food. I really wished that Candace had given me money now, as my stomach grumbled. It really wanted some nice greasy chips and mince in a bread roll. When I was in high school, I'd share the roll with Trudie and Pranish. But right now, I felt I could finish the entire thing myself. I rubbed my stomach. I hoped that wherever I found myself had plenty of free food.

I waited for a lull in the traffic and then crossed, sprinting across the road just as a van bleated its horn at me. Despite the relative banality of the act, it gave me a slight rush. I took a breath on the other side of the road and then moved down the alley.

A man stepped out in front of me, blocking my path. He had been standing behind the wall and Treth wouldn't have been able to see him.

I reached for my swords, and then noticed what he held in his hand. A pistol levelled right at me. Two more assailants peaked out from around the corner. I recognised them. The muggers from before. Well, some of them. The one with the ripped cheek had stitched it up with what seemed to be fishing line.

"That's her!" he said, spluttering.

"Nah, it was another girl with swords and a flaming coat," I replied, and then wanted to kick myself. I really didn't know how to be diplomatic.

"You put my bros in the alley-doc," the gunman said, pushing the pistol into my chest. My coat flared up, but it only caused him to press the pistol harder.

Chuffed as all hell, the other muggers moved closer.

"What's a bitch like you doing this far out in the slums, anyway?" the gunman asked. He seemed a bit more eloquent than his comrades.

"Hunting werewolves."

That gave them pause.

"Werewolf hunting?" the gun-man asked, incredulous. And then burst out laughing. The other muggers joined in but didn't seem to get the joke.

He stopped laughing and continued. "Werewolf hunting takes balls. Real balls. And you ain't got any."

"Careful," a voice came from behind my attackers. They turned. "If you knew who that was, you'd be afraid of losing your balls after talking to her like that."

"Guy!" I exclaimed. Never did I think I would see him in a place like this.

The gunman withdrew his pistol to point at Guy but paused as Guy levelled his dual machine-pistols at him and his friends.

"Here's the deal," Guy said. "You drop the pistol and any spare rounds you have, then beat it."

"Or?" the gunman said, defiantly.

"I either plant you here and now or let her cut your balls off."

I pressed my wakizashi to his throat from behind. A wonder how they had survived so long that they couldn't notice me drawing my sword.

"I'm fine with either option."

"Fine!" the gunman exclaimed, dropping his pistol with a clatter on the ground.

Guy approached closer, keeping his weapons trained on the gunman and the two other muggers.

I drew my dusack and pointed it at the other muggers, giving Guy an opening to pick up the dropped pistol. He inspected it.

"Not even loaded? You might as well have just used a knife."

Guy pocketed the pistol and indicated for the group to run.

"Beat it."

I let my sword drop from the gunman's throat and he was immediately away. The one with the cut cheek gave me a last look and I decided to give him a quick shallow slash across his back.

Guy looked at me.

"What?" I shrugged. "I didn't like him."

He looked me up and down. As if confirming that I was real.

"We've been searching for months," he said simply.

"And now you've found me," I replied, just as succinctly.

Slowly, he smiled, and holstered his pistols. I sheathed my swords and hugged him tightly.

"Where the hells have you been, Kat?" he asked.

"It's a long story."

"Months long, I presume."

I nodded. "Exactly. And best if I say it when everyone is around."

"Everyone?"

"I need your help. And Brett's. And anyone else that we can get."

"What's going on, Kat? Where have you been?"

"Guy," I said, avoiding his question. "What happened at the party? Do you know? Who died? Was Andy still turned?"

"Andy? Turned?" he paused and thought about the question. "We found evidence of a vampire attack. Three dead. You gone. Brett and I went tracking vampires for most of the time...but..."

He trailed off.

"It wasn't vampires," I replied. "What happened with Andy?"

"He wasn't there." Guy recalled something, and his expression saddened. "I'm sorry about Colin."

"Don't be. If you're gonna help me kill Andy."

"Andy? What?!"

"Do you have a car nearby? I've been walking for hours."

"Kat...why Andy? What happened?"

"I'll explain on the road. And can we stop for food?"

"Sure...sure."

Bemused, he led me down the alleyway to his car. He explained that he was actually back from a call-out when he saw the glow of my coat from behind and then rounded to flank the muggers.

Guy's van was pleasantly air-conditioned, and I sank into the upholstery, closing my eyes as I found myself feeling safe for the first time in a long while.

Guy started the engine and we began the drive.

"Guy," I said, after a period of silence. "Do you have a phone I can use? I'm a bit out-of-date with current events."

"Sure, Kat." He passed me his cell. It had a reinforced cover bearing the Drakenbane logo.

I switched accounts on his social media app to my account and checked through what I had missed. Hundreds of missed messages. Too many to reply to now. I scrolled past news articles on local elections, the call for the Necrolord investigation to stop, and news about the escalation of the war with the Sintari in New Zealand.

I stopped at a photo taken months back. Colin's profile. The last post he had ever made. A lame politics joke.

I didn't cry. But I wanted to.

Chapter 19. Reunion

Brett first looked at me like I was a ghost. But as my identity dawned on him, he muttered something and then charged me. I accepted his almost back-breaking hug and returned my own.

"I knew you weren't dead," he whispered, and I heard the pain in his voice, and a shock of my own misplaced guilt. What had I put him through? And why did that make me feel like this? Was it because I liked him? Or because Colin was dead, and I hadn't truly forgotten him yet. Or ever would. Brett's embrace lasted an age, and I didn't pull away. Or didn't want to pull away. It had been too long. And I owed it to my friends who sounded like they had tried everything to find me.

Guy had phoned ahead and told Brett to meet at Cindy's house. The first one to greet me was Alex, who surged out of Cindy's doorway to wind his way around my legs. Second was Duer, who glowed the warmest gold I've ever seen him glow, even as he said.

"Took ye long enough to get back!"

"Hi, Duer. I missed you too."

He glowed even brighter and landed on my shoulder. He smelled like vodka. Cindy must've been spoiling him.

Finally, there was the rendezvous with Brett. And somehow, it was the most intense of all.

After the heartfelt reunion, I sat down in Cindy's armchair as Guy insisted that I fill them in on what had happened. All three of them, the pixie and even my cat, waited with bated breath.

I sighed. "Best to start at the beginning. The party...vampires didn't kill Colin."

Cindy looked at Brett, with a look of vindication. He ignored her.

"It was..." I hesitated, but it had to come out. And I trusted these people. More than I trusted Pranish and Trudie. Because these fellow monster hunters would need to be the ones that helped me take my revenge. "Andy did it. He killed Colin just as the vampires attacked."

"How?" Cindy asked.

"He's a lycanthrope. Werewolf, I think. And must be an advanced one. He changed his arm to a claw at will..."

They all stared at me like I was mad.

"I'm not making things up!" I yelled, suddenly self-conscious that maybe I did make it up. "I saw him do it. Colin tried to defend himself, but the bullets didn't put him down."

Silence. Oh, Athena, was I insane?

"Colin's gun was empty," Guy said. "And there were spent shells around him. I just thought he was shooting at the vampires."

"The vampires came from another direction to where he was shooting," Cindy added, holding her chin thoughtfully.

"I believe you, Kat," Brett said. "And we'll put the son of a bitch down."

"Hasty, aren't we?" Cindy chided, but sighed. "It's not like we're in the evidence game. And if he is a werewolf, he isn't protected by the Spirit of the Law."

"My question still stands, though," Guy added. "Where have you been?"

He looked more closely at me.

"And why the hells are your eyes two different colours?"

Cindy and Brett seemed to only notice now. Duer flew up to my face for a closer look and then shrugged. Didn't seem so odd to him.

Now was the hard part.

"I've been…with the Necrolord."

"What?!" they all said in unison.

"Did you escape?"

"What did she do to you?"

"The eye? Why the eye?"

"Please, please…" I held up my hand to hold back their questions. I felt Candace watching with interest.

"Kat," Cindy asked, quietly now that the others had quietened. "You've been gone for months. How did you escape after so long?"

"I didn't escape," I said. "She released me…"

"Why would she do that?" Cindy's tone had the undeniable hint of mistrust in it. Treth liked it.

"Because…" How would they take this? "We became friends."

I felt a warm feeling from Candace and displeasure from Treth as the three monster hunters stared at me in disbelief.

259

"Kat...she's a necromancer. She killed so many people," Cindy said, looking at me like I had Stockholm Syndrome. Maybe I did?

"It's not that simple. She's a victim in this. And she helped me. She stopped the vampires at the party and got me out. Kept me hidden from Charlene Terhoff and the Conclave."

"Conclave?" Cindy asked.

"A secret society. Candace says they were the ones behind Jeremiah Cox, the Blood Cartel and Digby."

"Sounds very convenient."

"But it makes sense! Digby had handlers, and we already suspected that the Blood Cartel and Jeremiah were connected to something larger. They were too powerful, too swift in their rise, to just be lone agents."

They all didn't look like they believed me. Even Alex looked dubious. All except Brett. He looked...still disbelieving that I was even there.

I sighed. "I know what it must sound like. That I've been brainwashed. But Cindy, you should be able to check that. Can you detect any curses or corruption on me?"

She cracked her fingers together and held them on my head and breast. She muttered a few words. I felt nothing, but her eyes looked shocked for a second, and then she withdrew her hands.

"You're clean...except for something very peculiar. I think it's time to spill the beans about that hazel eye."

"It's Candace's."

"Candace?"

"The Necrolord."

"You have the Necrolord's eye?!" It was Brett's turn to look shocked.

"She's suffering from a form of madness brought on by using dark magic and light magic simultaneously." I spoke fast, to avoid any interruptions. "But by feeling my presence, the madness is kept at bay. I made the deal with her of my own volition, so I could come and kill Andy."

"And what then?" Brett asked. He sounded...hurt. I didn't know why.

"Then, Colin will be avenged. A monster will be slain. And that should be good enough. That's our fucking job, after all. The pay-check is just a bonus. None of us do this for the money. You can make more working for

261

Sanitation. And that's much less dangerous. We all do this because we've realised that there're creatures in this world which need to be removed. And with or without you, I am going to go and slay a monster."

A pause followed my speech. They stared at me, not so disbelieving but with a hint of awe, worry and disbelief on all their faces.

"Fine!" Brett said, standing up. "I already agreed to do it. You in?"

He looked at Guy.

"Gods, you've got to be fucking kidding me," Guy answered. "First vampires and now a werewolf kid?"

Brett kept staring at him. Guy sighed.

"Yeah, fuck. I'm in."

"You idiots might need a healer," Cindy added. "And while not all werewolves are bad, Andy has never been my cup of tea."

I looked at them and was only able to mutter out a quiet but truly sincere.

"Thank you."

The room turned into a cacophony as everyone moved to start preparing. Guy and Brett got on the phone to some buddies and Cindy went to prepare some scrolls. A thought occurred to me and I asked Cindy if I could use her phone. She handed me mine, saying that Brett retrieved my bag from the party.

I was just about to phone Trudie but stopped. What would she think? I just came back from the dead and wanted to kill her boyfriend. That was too much to lay on my friend. At least, not yet.

No, I couldn't let Trudie know I killed Andy. I loved her, but I wasn't sure she could comprehend my reasons. Or truly understand what he did.

Instead, I phoned Pranish.

"Who the fuck is calling with this number?" Pranish yelled, only two rings in.

"Love you too, Pranish."

"Holy fuck, Kat!" He sounded in between fainting and crying. "We thought you were dead!"

"Everyone can be wrong once in their life. How are things?"

"How are things? Fucking fine. Arjun got me disinherited. But DigiLaw got signed on by Shard's biggest

263

competitor. I didn't receive a Christmas card from the family, as to be expected. And…"

He paused.

"Fuck, Kat. I don't know if you know, but…"

"Colin's dead. I know."

"I'm sorry…"

"Don't be. Andy did it."

"What?!"

"Andy's a werewolf. He killed Colin before the vamps attacked. We're gonna go kill him. You in?"

He paused, before whispering his reply.

"Kat, I don't know what happened to you these past months, but I believe you. The thing is…I just can't do it. Again, that is. I…remember the last time. And, I can't put myself through it this time. I'm sorry."

"I understand, Pranish. I do. Just, do me a favour and not tell Trudie I'm back until everything is sorted. I'm killing her boyfriend, after all."

"Of course, Kat. And you've got my support in this. Good luck."

"Thanks. See you around."

I hung up just as he was about to speak. Probably just a goodbye. I was disappointed that he wasn't coming to help, but I understood. We were all different. Pranish did his time in the trenches. And while I may keep coming back, it wasn't my right to send him over the top.

"Kat," Brett said, cradling a paperbag with something in it. "I believe this is yours."

I accepted the package and opened it. It was Voidshot. My enchanted Mauser pistol. I looked at Brett as my way of thanks. He smiled, faintly.

"It's good to have you back…Katty."

Chapter 20. Knock-knock

Brett and Guy managed to get a good bunch of people to come and help. Some of the guys brought even more guys with them. When I saw the group of hunters pledged to help me storm Andy's manor and put him down, my first thought was my bank balance. When I said as much, Hammond – the pyromancer that I'd saved by cutting off his infected arm – stated that they were doing this *pro bono*.

"For the sake of community service," he said, with a toothy grin.

"The real reason?" I asked Brett.

"You saved them," he said. "The cops might not like you, but almost every hunter who went raiding with you knows that if they needed help, you'd be there. They're here to return the favour."

"We're doing an unsanctioned raid on the house of a Councillor," I added, at risk of putting the group off.

"Never liked Councillors," Hammond replied. Some of his friends from Puretide, now wearing unmarked black combat gear, nodded.

"And if the Councillor's son is a werewolf, then we've got the right to make a citizen's arrest," Busani, a Drakenbane operator, added.

"We're killing him…" Brett replied, dubious.

Busani shrugged. "Potato, tomato. Same difference."

In total, the group to storm the manor would be me, Brett, Guy, Cindy, Hammond and five others from Drakenbane and Puretide. Ten in total. Would it be enough? I sure hoped so, seeing that I was planning on doing this alone if necessary.

We left the parking garage we had used for the meet. Hammond caught up with me at the front.

"What's with the eyes, boss?"

"Long story."

"Long drive."

"Would you believe me if I said it's the eye of the Necrolord?"

"Nope." He grinned, lit a cigarette and fell back in line with his Puretide buddies.

***

Night. The moon shone through the treetops, forming silver dagger tips off the moisture that clung to the leaves.

The approach to the Garce Manor was defended by a stretch of pine trees coming down from the mountain. We took a hiking trail to make our way to the back. Andy lived in a rich area. It enjoyed easy access to some of the remaining legal hiking trails on Table Mountain and a decent view of the ocean. Rather than make me regret that I didn't pursue my relationship with him, his display of wealth made me hate him more. And I was very much a capitalist. It made me hate him because even if he wasn't a monster, his wealth highlighted his weakness. His dad was a politician. Making money for doing practically nothing. The Garces never had to struggle. Never really had to look death in the eye. They had no skin in the game. Took no risks. No. They just took from everyone else.

But now it was our turn to take from them.

Brett signed for his flank to proceed forward. The lights were on in the manor and I could see the yellow glow reflect off the silver of Brett's axe. The one he had sent a picture of to me months back. The one I had been disturbed by. Because I had Colin, then. Peaceful Colin. Capable, yet gentle. The Colin who had been aghast at the idea that he would need to kill somebody. But accepted it anyway. Because I insisted, he took the pistol that had failed to save his life. Brett was not gentle. He was not Colin. He did not balk at the kill. And neither did I.

I glanced behind me. Cindy was pulling up the rear. She looked poised. Calm. She was stretching her fingers and muttering incantations. I was glad to have her onboard. There was no one else more capable of keeping us all alive.

Surrounding Andy's manor was a spiked wall. Nothing fancy like an electric fence. We were coming from the mountain. Biggest threat, besides some freak rift-borne monster, would be a baboon trying to jump the wall to steal food. Hammond's flank on the right moved in front of us, while we took cover behind rocks and the treeline. He walked nonchalantly up to the wall, glancing at the manor on the other side. Looking for something to indicate a security camera. He seemed satisfied and indicated that Brett's flank should advance. That left my flank in the centre. Much to my chagrin, the group wanted to protect me, and put me in the support group with Cindy and a Shield-Mage. Jokes on them. When the fighting started, I was breaking rank and finding Andy for myself.

One of Hammond's buddies lifted him up so he could peer over the wall. He gripped one of the spikes in his hand and I watched it glow red-hot. He then carefully squished it flat. He did this with a few more of the spikes, and then motioned to be lowered to the ground. I advanced as Hammond did an exaggerated theatrical bow, allowing Brett to take the lead.

Brett complied, even as I felt a pang of fear that he was leading the attack. But I didn't voice it. Even if I had lost so many people already. I was so close. I could even feel both Treth's and Candace's excitement. If only Treth knew how similar the sense of Candace in my head was to how I felt him. I hoped he would come to accept her, in time.

Brett disappeared over the wall. Guy followed. Busani next. One by one, the group passed over the wall. Only one of Hammond's Puretide breachers stayed. He would blow up the wall if necessary, to allow us a quick getaway. He helped me over the wall before Cindy.

I was relieved to find all my comrades still in one piece, taking cover in the foliage in Andy's expansive backyard. Some were hiding behind a pool-house, while others were lying prone behind bushes. Brett was crouched, waiting for me. He brought his mouth close to my ear and whispered.

"Let us fight any guards. You focus on the prize."

I barely noted what he said, as his warm breath on my ear sent a tingle down my spine.

I scolded myself. This was not the time. I remembered Colin. And then Andy. Anger replaced the tingle.

I nodded.

Cindy came over the wall, landing with a little less grace than the rest of us, but still maintaining her poise.

Brett signed to the group and we made our way to the backdoor of the manor. Everything was quiet from inside, despite the lights being on. Was he home? I hoped so. Imagining the awkwardness of invading his house just to find him absent was a bit too embarrassing. And frustrating!

Hammond's flank took a position at the corner of the manor, watching the side alley. Brett's and my flank proceeded to the sliding glass backdoor.

I placed my ear on the glass, unable to see through to the other side because of the curtains. I heard nothing.

I almost jumped as I heard a branch crack. I turned behind us. Nobody else seemed to have noticed. I peered back towards the wall we had scaled. At the tree-tops on the other side.

The others were looked through windows, trying to get any sense of the internal layout before we attacked. I continued looking behind us.

Cindy noticed my behaviour and leant in to whisper.

"What is it?"

A corpse dropped a metre away from us just as she finished, splattering onto the hard ground. I felt blood spray all over me. Some hissed on my coat. It was the breacher we had left behind, and his face was torn into an eternal scream.

The group fanned out, holding their weapons facing every which way, even as the breacher's friend crouched down, not believing his friend was dead.

We all heard the growl. It didn't sound like it was from an animal. Or any monster I'd ever faced. It sounded elemental. Like the wind. And it rumbled from the roof above us. Two yellow eyes glinted in the moonlight and the creature didn't move as torches were shone on it. It was hunched over, crossed between standing on all fours like a beast, yet ready to pounce like a man-hunter. Its maw was distinctly canine, yet no wolf I had ever seen bore that many bloodied teeth. And no wolf I had ever seen had that look of truly human hatred in its eyes.

We heard a cry just as the Shield-Mage was pulled into the pool. The water turned red, and a soaked werewolf leapt out from its hiding place. He shook off pool water and innards and let out a deep growl.

Hammond's flank had closed ranks. His hand was glowing a fiery orange. I felt heat emanate from it.

I had drawn Voidshot and my wakizashi. The blade of the latter began to glow a flaming orange as Hammond incanted something onto it. I may not have a silver sword, but fire hurt wolves just as much.

"Kat," Brett whispered, loudly. "Get inside with Cindy. We'll hold them off."

I was about to reply.

"Don't give me that, '*I can't leave you behind*'. Go!"

"I was gonna say thanks," I said.

The group closed ranks around me. I stabbed the lock of the door with my super-heated sword and then forced it to slide open. As I entered, my comrades released a salvo of shots, followed by roars and screaming.

The house was still quiet, even as any sound would have been drowned out by the cacophony outside. Cindy didn't say anything, but I saw her glancing behind her. She wanted to be there. To keep her friends safe.

"Go back, Cindy. I can handle myself."

"You're our priority, Kat."

"And you are all mine. Go keep them safe."

She looked about to argue, but then nodded and turned back. The biggest fight was there. I didn't need a healer right now.

"Alone again," Treth said.

"I'm never alone."

He nodded. "I know. In fact, it is starting to feel a bit crowded in here."

I made my way through the house, past a lounge area with a flat-screen that took up the entire wall, and a room with its own pool table. Past rooms filled with bunkbeds. This didn't only look like the house of a rich boy, it looked like a barracks. That would explain the multiple werewolves.

I came to a staircase, which I began to climb. It would seem right for Andy to live on the second storey. Some sort of domination complex. Hells, I really was demonising the guy. But I was hopefully fast approaching killing him, so did that really matter?

"You know…" a voice behind me said, causing me to level Voidshot down the staircase, pointing straight at Oliver's head. "I'm not a fan of cats."

He grinned, that arrogant idiot grin. His eyes glowed yellow but he was in human form. I fired and he nimbly dodged out of the way, letting the round embed itself in the ground floor.

"That must make me a stereotype," he said. "A canine who hates felines. But who can blame me? When the cat won't do what it's fucking told."

"I saw you die!" I answered, just as I fired again. This round sailed past his head and into a vase.

"You've made mistakes before, Kat."

It was subtle, but his muscles were growing larger. And were his teeth growing sharper? And longer?

"Mistake number one. Not minding your own business."

His face started to sprout fur.

"Mistake number two. Denying your own true happiness with my alpha."

His shirt began to rip, with furred muscle appearing underneath. His arms lengthened, grotesquely, as he was caught between man and monster.

"Mistake number three," he growled, his voice rumbling. "Underestimating…"

I caught him mid-sentence as I jumped from my higher step and brought my sword down on him. His eyes were bemused, just as my blade bit into his shoulder blade and slid right to his nipple. The impact of my legs hitting the ground shocked my knees, but also caused him to fall to the ground. I pulled my blade out, just as he tried to swipe at me with a partly formed werewolf claw. I side-stepped and brought my sword back for a thrust. The blade found its mark right between his eyes. The flames cauterised the wounds immediately, preventing them from regenerating. Who needed silver when you just burnt their wounds?

Oliver's face was caught in a half-wolf/half-human snarl. I pulled out my blade. His flesh bubbled and smelled like burnt meat. With a clean swipe, I took off his head.

"Now, who am I supposed to not underestimate?"

"Pretty sure he's dead," Treth said. "He can't hear you."

"I was being dramatic."

"Time and place, Kat. Let's get this over with so we can get this eye out of our…your head."

"You believe her now?"

"I believe that she is mad, but honest."

"Babysteps." I smiled. "Glad we're getting on the same page."

"Far from it. Plenty of villains are honest. It's not an overwhelming virtue."

"Well, back to the drawing board."

Treth grunted.

From the top of the stairway, the sound of fighting outside was a dull buzz. Was the house soundproofed? That was suspicious. I really doubted it was to drown out the noises of the city. I was much more convinced that its purpose was to keep sounds from escaping the house.

I ensured my footfalls were steady and quiet, keeping Voidshot and my flaming sword pointed in either direction. Werewolves, despite their bestial nature, or rather because of it, were sneaky bastards. My coat still maintained its errant glow. It was excited. Could it feel the kill approaching? Did it relish it just as much as I? And what did that mean for me that I felt the same thing as a dead salamander's hide?

I chose to ignore the thought, as I arrived at a closed door, with light escaping through a gap below. I took a deep breath, waiting by the side of the door, and then kicked it wide open.

My gun was immediately levelled at Andy, who was lying in his underwear (mercifully) on a queen-sized bed with a red duvet. His shock at seeing me was brief and was replaced almost instantaneously with joy.

"I was wondering what was making all that noise. I thought it was just the boys having fun. But now I see that they have some new toys."

"I could just pull the trigger now," I said. "I almost always do. But this time, I thought…make him suffer."

"Kat?" the voice I heard shot me right through the heart, as I turned to see Trudie exiting the bathroom, wearing black lingerie, leaving little to the imagination.

"Trudie!" I almost shouted. "I can explain!"

Trudie buckled at the knees, tears welled up in her eyes.

"I…thought you were dead."

My eyes were fixed on my best friend, even as my pistol was pointed at Andy.

"I…I can explain…"

She looked at me, up and down. At the blood staining my face, shirt and pants. At my flaming cloak. And at the gun pointed at her boyfriend.

"What…what's…"

In a flash, Andy had pounced, belting her across the face. She fell to the ground, blood oozing from a gash on her cheek. I hesitated at his speed and tried to fire. The bullet didn't come close to hitting him. I felt a searing pain in my hand as he grabbed onto my wrist, forcing Voidshot out of my hand. He did the same to my other hand. I was winded as he knocked me to the ground, pressing his knees into my thighs, and holding my arms to the ground. I struggled, and my coat flared, igniting his carpet, but he didn't budge.

"You're alive!" he cried, like an excited puppy. "Oh, how excited I am to finally be able to rid myself of that witch. Her incessant nattering. Her girliness and weakness. The only thing that could make me stomach her was your scent around her. But it's been too long. Too long without you. She wasn't smelling like you anymore. But she was all I had left of you. My perfect, perfect Kat."

His eyes glowed yellow, but not the angry yellow I'd seen in Oliver's. His eyes were filled with unbridled lust.

"You killed her!" I screamed, as I struggled against his monstrous grip. "You killed him!"

I felt Treth's desperation, searching for a way out. I also felt his hate for this man, and his worry over Trudie. Candace was curious, yet worried about me. But I felt a confidence. She believed I'd get out of this. I wasn't so sure, as I felt his hot, rapid breaths on my face.

"She can take a little bit of a hit, my dear Kat. I wouldn't kill your friends, would I? Only that…menace. But that's because you wouldn't see reason. He was weak. And you are strong. You deserve someone just as strong as you are."

"You're not strong, you fucking monster." I spat. "The strong don't go crazy when they can't get what they want. The strong can control themselves. You're a mindless beast!"

I winced as his grip tightened on my wrists. And he hadn't even transformed yet.

"Shush, my sweet. We have all night to talk. All night for our reunion. No more pretending. No more ruses to make you jealous. You are mine now. And even if you can't see it, I'll make you mine."

The door swung open, revealing one of Brett's Drakenbane buddies. He looked shocked just as he levelled his gun at Andy. Too late. With a roar, Andy was across the room, his arm transformed into a furred claw. He ripped out the man's innards, pulling out his intestines and letting blood pool on the floor. Through the open door, I heard more fighting. Howls. Gunshots. Shouting. And I smelled fire. Burnt flesh and fur.

I managed to pull myself to my feet, just as the man fell to the ground. Andy charged me, pinning me to the wall. His breathing was hot. Excited. He pressed his body up against mine and I felt sick that I had thought I had ever liked him.

"I have waited to turn you since we met. The waiting was agony. You know how difficult it is to chain the wolf within? It bites at your very soul. But he is content now. He knows that our time has come. And you will have your own wolf…"

Own wolf in my head? Alongside Treth and Candace? Treth was right. It was getting crowded.

But my jests aside, I couldn't breathe. He licked my neck, and I noticed that his teeth were distinctly long and canine. I gagged and he laughed.

"A werewolf named Kat." He grinned and I saw his canines growing. "Wait until my father hears about this…"

I kicked against him and my coat, reacting to my anger and fear, scorched the wall, and his hands. He didn't seem to care about the burns. I struggled, impotently. He seemed to enjoy every moment of it. But there was no way out. I was going to be turned. A fate, I am unsure was worse than that of the dead man, his intestines pooled before him.

I stopped, suddenly, as I heard Candace's voice in my head. But it wasn't English. It was guttural. It was painful. It spewed darkness.

"No," I thought to her, and said it aloud. The meekness in my voice seemed to excite Andy further as he pressed closer towards me, swatting at my flaming coat to get access to the clothes underneath.

She continued, her spoken words becoming scratchy symbols inside my mind. Symbols that exuded an eternity of pain and death.

"I can't. I must not. I'm not a necromancer!"

Andy reached down towards my pants. Treth felt hopeless. Guilty. Desperate. But Candace overwhelmed his presence, and the words passed through my lips.

Andy paused, as Candace spoke the spell through me, and then opened his mouth wide, extending his growing maw over my neck. The words infested my every pore, but Candace overwhelmed my sense of revulsion. She became one with me. Not master. Not puppeteer. She became…me.

He cried out as the dead man's teeth sank into his neck. I felt a profound relief as his body pulled away from mine. He swiped at the zombie and the force of the blow split the zombie in half. It was the delay I needed and I grabbed my fallen sword, its flames now extinguished. But I felt Candace's limited control over Andy's body as his veins filled with necro-blood, vying for dominance over his lycanthropy.

"I said I would make you suffer," I panted, holding my sword aloft, as his body was caught in the throes of transformation and his approach into zombification. I would not let him last long enough to see which won out. As much as I wanted him to feel every ounce of pain he had caused, and more. Fortunate for him that I needed his blood before it became black.

He looked at me now the way he should have. The way monsters were meant to. Yellow eyes of rage. Not lust. This was the way it was meant to be. I looked him in the eyes, as his flesh roiled, hair sprouting and falling off in phases as the rot set in and was fought back by his regeneration. I didn't want to be merciful. But I had a job to do. Always the job. He was a monster. And I was a hunter.

I slit his throat and watched the blood spray. He let out a gargled and mournful howl. His regeneration halted and I felt Candace release her control over him.

I drew an empty plastic water bottle from my inner jacket pocket and held it to catch the blood. It managed to fill to the brim. I felt Candace's satisfaction and then closed the bottle.

He collapsed and I saw no movement. He was dead.

Without immediate danger, I heard the cacophony of gunfire and sirens. But my attention was focused on the eviscerated man whom I had risen.

"What have I done?"

"What I feared," Treth hissed. "I knew this would happen!"

Brett burst in, covered in blood and matted chunks of fur. He had a bloodied axe in his one hand and one of Guy's pistols in his other.

"Kat!" he shouted, relieved. He glanced down at Andy, dead and malformed. And then at the dead zombie. I hoped he didn't figure anything out. Not until I knew exactly what had happened. And maybe not even then.

I saw my friend, still on the floor, and rushed to her. She still had a pulse! Oh, I was ready to praise Athena, Odin and even blighted Anubis for that.

"Are you hurt?" Brett, touched my shoulder. The coat didn't burn him.

"I'm fine!" I snapped. "Help me lift her."

He stowed his weapons and picked her up in both arms.

"What happened?" I asked, smelling the fire worsen. I made my way to the door and retrieved Voidshot, hoping he wouldn't see the details of my kill.

"After we killed the wolves, Whiteshield showed up. Fucking Whiteshield."

"Councillor house. To be expected."

"Poor fucking Todd." Brett shook his head. I must have imagined his suspicion before. Todd's zombie corpse didn't look undead.

"Let's get out of here."

Brett nodded and followed me as I took the lead. We passed Hammond shooting a jet of flames down the hall, bullets passing just over his head. Cindy was crouched over Guy, who was holding his stomach as blood pooled onto the floor. She furrowed her brow as gold erupted from her fingertips and Guy's cheeks didn't look so sallow any more.

"You kill him, boss?" Hammond asked through gritted teeth as he held up the onslaught of flames against the gunmen.

"He's dead," I answered, bluntly. "Can you cover our retreat?"

"Can fucking do that, boss. And that kill better be worth it. I'm gonna have to tell Rupie's mom he's dead."

That stung. It stung hard. But I turned my back on him and ran. Cindy helped Guy to his feet and Busani helped steady her. She must have used up a lot of her spark.

We met with others at the end of the hallway. They fired a few shots out the smashed window.

"We're going, lads!" Brett yelled. They didn't delay jumping out the window.

I heard cries from behind us and then heard Hammond running towards us.

"Run!"

We followed the men outside the window. My knees buckled on impact and I stopped to help Brett hand Trudie down. Whiteshield operatives flanked from around the alley and I fired on them with Voidshot. The first round hit the first man squarely in the head. He fell. The second and third shot sent his friends into cover. Another human kill for me. Was making a habit out of it. Chalk it up to my continual descent into darkness. Treth had a point.

Cindy was last to jump down. Guy, with his renewed strength, caught her. As a group, we ran towards the treeline. The wall from before had been blown up, concrete rubble strewn across the yard.

The trees were cover, and I willed my coat to darken as we rushed towards it. Brett passed me, carrying Trudie. He passed the trees and I felt relief. Just as the manor exploded, incinerating everything it held within and all evidence of my necromancy. The flames shot out like a fireball.

Brett turned and cried out. I wasn't far enough away. The flames hit me and I felt pain. And then...nothing.

Chapter 21. Family

I dreamed of my parents dying. But they weren't my parents. It was a man and woman I had never seen before, but that I knew to be my mom and dad. But the man who killed them was not the man who killed my parents. It was another dressed the same. And as I stood in a dark room, screaming and crying, a man dressed in black offered me a chance to bring them back. To bring them all back. But I knew that he had already taken everything from me.

***

I awoke to a pair of yellow eyes. Not animalistic, like a werewolf, but rather the sickly artificialness of a homunculus. Swirling with unnaturalness. Petunia watched me as only a curious child could. She recoiled, backing away slightly and resting on her knuckles as I gasped, sitting upright.

Candace held a syringe and a bottle of amber liquid. I didn't know what it was, and I didn't want to know. Her white rubber gloves were covered in red.

"Are you feeling any pain?" she asked.

"The fire? The explosion? Whiteshield?" I went off and looked around the room. It was just us. In Candace's lab. "Where are my friends?"

"I saved you from the fire. Your coat absorbed much of it, but even then, you had burns too severe for any normal human to survive."

I gritted my teeth and with newfound anger, turned on the necromancer.

"Where are my friends?"

"There, somewhere…" she shrugged. "It doesn't matter. What matters is that we are together again. And we can finally begin…"

I shook my head, still groggy.

"Begin what?"

Her eyes lit up and she placed down her apparatus and took off her bloodied gloves.

"Begin the end, Kat. The end of the madness. The end of the darkness. And we shall be with them. And I will finally be able to see again."

Her tone made me distinctly uncomfortable, but I saw the quiver of her lip. The uncertainty showing through the shaking of her hand. She was human. She was a child.

"I started this," I whispered, to Treth and to myself. "I might as well see it to the end."

I felt Treth consider my words. He nodded, even so I sensed his reluctance. That is all I could ask. Not that he accepted my decisions, not yet. But that he would hear me out. When this was all over.

I took a deep breath. I pushed aside the thoughts of the flames. Of my friends looking back at me as the flames shot out. And I tried to forget the thought of my vengeance. But I realised there was nothing left to agonise about. Andy was dead. Colin was avenged. Why then did I feel so empty?

I had only this left.

Candace. And a question I needed answered:

Was I wrong? Was everything wrong?

"Are you ready?" I asked, just as Candace paled, staring off into the abyss.

"What is it?" I asked. She didn't have a hint of madness about her.

"It can't be," she muttered. "The sun is coming in just an hour or two. They wouldn't risk it."

"What is it?" I repeated, but I could guess.

"Vampires," she said, simply.

"They're here for me. I'll hold them off."

"No! I need you to be there…with me."

I took her in my arms.

"I will be. But you need to see if you're right. I brought them here. I'll fight them. And then when you are ready, call me through the eye to bring me to the site."

Candace sniffed, but nodded. I released her and squeezed her shoulder.

"It's the beginning of the end," I said. "But whatever happens, you are my friend."

"No." She smiled. "Sisters."

I smiled back. "Yes. Sisters."

The sound of breaching explosives signalled the end of our soppy rendezvous.

"Go! Bring back your parents," I said.

She turned and made her way to the ritual site.

"And Candy…"

She stopped.

"I'm ready to fight by your army's side now."

She paused and nodded. At once, I heard a gut-wrenching roar and the thundering of a hundred undead. Perhaps more. Candace was gone, off to finish her ritual.

"I never thought I would fight side by side with the undead," Treth said.

"Neither did I."

"Are you still sure about her, Kat?"

"The surest I've ever been. Because I need to know. And because she deserves to try."

"I don't agree with this…" he muttered. "I don't agree with the way she invaded your mind and pushed those words through your mouth."

"She saved us."

"I know."

But at what cost? Was left unspoken.

"We'll get to all that," I said, lifting my coat around my shoulders. It warmed in greeting. And did it feel a bit warmer than usual? It must have enjoyed the inferno that almost killed me. I buckled my sword belt and sheathed my swords. My wakizashi was still bloodied. I looked at it, crusty with werewolf blood. And then at my dusack. Clean. I hadn't used it in an age. Neither would be that effective against vampires. In the long run, at least. Without silver, their flesh would knit back together. But I could still behead them. Slow them down. Keep them from Candace.

Five more silver rounds for Voidshot. I wished Candace had retrieved more, but she was out of resources. No more cash. Just her last garrison of walking corpses. No longer the Necrolord. Another reason not to kill her.

"We can do this, Kat," Treth said, sensing my trepidation.

I sheathed both my swords and held my pistol aloft. I rubbed the inscription. German. I didn't understand it. I didn't need to. I holstered it.

"We always have, Treth. And we'll do it again. And again. Together. Down the same path, to darkness and into the abyss of chaos."

"Hopefully not that far."

I smiled and walked towards the sound of battle. It sounded like a place I belonged.

***

Three bullets left. First missed. Second planted a vamp long enough for me to remove his head. His body was still moving. I let the zombies have it. The twisting hallways of

Candace's stronghold, the ones I had feared and become so claustrophobic in before, were now my domain. The undead travelled easily in the darkness. As easily as the vampires. But they had a distinct advantage. They could feel no fear. No shock. They knew their master's domain as well as she did. And I was only to follow them to the slaughter.

Ghouls led the assault. Grey-skinned bestial men and women hit a tide of rotting, writhing carcasses. They bit. They clawed. Blood didn't spray. But flesh flew. And there was gnawing. And bone snapping. I stayed away from the melee, searching for my own – more intelligent – prey. The zombies eventually overwhelmed their vampiric counterparts. Ghouls needed blood to thrive, of which the zombies had only toxic blood to provide. Zombies needed only flesh. Ghouls, despite their curse, had more than enough flesh for the ravenous dead.

The battle continued. Throughout the complex. And I fought side by side with my sworn enemy.

A vampire was strong. Twenty zombies were stronger. I did not delight in realising this. Because I didn't know which I hated more. But the zombies were on my side, at least this time. I moved just behind them, letting them take the brunt of vampire attackers. When they couldn't handle it, I swooped in and attacked.

"You thirsty, leach?" I coaxed the vamp before me, holding my wakizashi and my smoking Voidshot. The vamp clutched his wounded shoulder. Smoke rose from the bullet hole and the flesh wasn't stitching up.

He snarled, just as a zombie bit into his leg. He raised his sword and parried the attack of another. I let the zombies have their fun, giving myself a breather.

"Ceiling," Treth warned.

I fired Voidshot straight up and was rewarded with droplets of blood. I backed off as the vamp fell to the floor. Two zombies turned on it, but it was fast, and managed to behead both of them with its dual meat-cleavers. Cleanly, in a half pirouette. I had to admit that I liked the vamp's form. It was similar to mine.

He ignored his comrade's cries of pain as he was mobbed by the undead and faced me. He held his one blade aloft, pointed at me in challenge.

"You slew kin," he said, simply. His words sounded forced. Rehearsed. His accent was very different from his choice of words.

"Is it vampire culture to be pretentious?"

He snarled and, in a black and white flash, charged me. I saw strands of my hair cut loose as I ducked down and drove my sword into his belly. His face was just above my coat and even without my conscious will, the coat ignited and spewed flames into his face. I twisted the blade as the jets of flame scorched him, and then shoved him off my blade.

He fell to the ground. The hole in his belly started to stitch up immediately, but the bullet hole in his thigh was still smoking. His face was blistering, with black pustules spewing blood. His lips and all his hair were seared off. He still moved.

Before he could rise, I charged and arced my blade to take off his head. His cleaver rose and deflected my blade. My arm rang from the blow and I backed off. He rose, like the undead. I realised that his eyes weren't closed. His eyelids had been incinerated, alongside the eyes on the other side. He looked like a zombie.

A real zombie charged him from behind. He sidestepped it and nimbly slashed its head off in a clean blow. As if cutting butter.

He rasped something at me. But the fire in his lungs didn't let any comprehensible words escape.

I didn't charge him immediately. And Candace must have seen what I did, as her zombies backed off, creating a circle to block his escape. I was glad for that. I didn't want them to live, exactly, but with how few they were left, they were not as expendable. The flesh puppets were even more valuable, but I couldn't rely on Candace to control them effectively while she was conducting the ritual.

"We are lucky he wasn't with the rest," Treth commented, referencing the solo vampires we had mobbed and killed earlier.

I paced, side to side, watching him. He stood still, holding his cleavers steady. His head didn't follow me. Could he hear? Could he smell? How did he know?

I holstered Voidshot and picked up a dismembered zombie head. I tossed it at him. He cut it in two.

I backed away, out of surprise, and he charged me. I felt the cleaver scrape into my upper arm and my coat shoot fire in response. I stabbed in his direction while simultaneously spinning to avoid his other cleaver. I hit the wall of the corridor behind me and just managed to draw my dusack to deflect another blow from his cleaver. My dusack chipped and my arm gave way under his vampiric strength. It fell and the blade of the cleaver managed to nick my shoulder.

I winced but rebounded with a thrust from my wakizashi. It pierced his stomach. I twisted the blade and slashed, disembowelling him. Candace's zombies pounced on him, pulling him backwards and away from me. I stood and tried to raise my wounded arm. I still could, even though it hurt. The zombies munched on the vampire's limbs and neck, as he swatted at them with his cleavers as if they were flies.

I rounded to his side and slashed at his ankles. He fell to his knees. The zombies on his neck moved to the rest of his body, giving me an opening. Targeting the fleshy dents in his neck, I slashed, taking his head off. A zombie picked it up and began eating it even as the mouth still moved and the eyelids grew back.

Silver, sunlight, purification and fire were the only ways to kill a vampire effectively. That, and eating them alive, it seemed.

I looked down the long hallway, still hearing the undead fight further in the stronghold. I tried to move my feet, but my vision blurred. I lent up against the wall, panting, while listening to the grotesque feast at my side.

"Kat…" a voice echoed inside my head. I focused. It was Candace. I saw a vision of what she saw. A circular room. Two corpses. Graffscripp and healing runes written in silver dust and dark blood.

"It is ready, sister. Be here."

I saw out of my own eye again. The zombies silently charged to battle. The vampire was just bones now.

"Time to end this," I said. I was shocked by my own voice. I sounded…scared.

"One way or another," Treth replied.

I backtracked down the dark halls, towards the lab. The corpses of zombies and the forward vamp scouts were like breadcrumbs to guide me out of the forest. The dining room door was open, and the fire was lit, as per usual.

I jogged through the door and was winded as something knocked me to the ground. Petunia lay on top of me. Her back was bristling with spikes. Blood was seeping into her shirt.

I felt a stab of pain in Candace's eye. She screamed.

I pushed Petunia off me and drew Voidshot, firing in a single movement. The shot hit the vampire in the head. It fell into the fire and screamed as it burnt alive.

Petunia was gasping when I got to her. I cradled her in my arms, keeping the blades from touching the ground. Yet I saw the tips peeking out through the front of her shirt.

"Ka…." she tried to say, blinking away tears.

"It's okay, Petunia. Everything is going to be okay."

She looked like she believed me, even as her eyes greyed and she rasped. "So—rreee."

Her breathing stopped and her eyes lost their swirl. I closed her eyelids and laid her down.

I ran the rest of the way to the ritual room. When I saw Candace, she was pale.

"I can bring her back. After this."

I nodded. Not sure if I believed her.

"Bar the door. I can't rely on flesh-puppets to hold any more of them off."

I noticed the dismembered corpse of a vampire in the corner. The flesh-puppets, still as statues, had blood on their weapons. I barred the door and, after I did so, the

301

flesh-puppets collapsed, like ragdolls. I stood next to the door, my swords drawn.

Candace took her spot alongside her parents. They looked serene. All their wounds had been stitched up. If not for the complete lack of movement, they could have just been sleeping.

"First," she announced. "To bring back the souls of the departed. And to summon them back from beyond the In Between."

Candace drew a knife and cut her palm. I winced as she sprinkled the blood onto her father's and then her mother's forehead.

"The true names of the fallen," she continued, using her bloodied hand to shape the spilled blood into symbols. "Richardson Mount Evergreen – and Thyrene Leturn."

She stopped and put her bloody handprint over both their lips.

"The soul is bound. As it should be. As your time is not yet over."

She deposited the knife on a table and drew a bouquet of daffodils. She closed her eyes and whispered words that sounded similar to that of Cindy's. She was a healer. She could heal!

The daffodils disintegrated into a golden mist and seeped into the mouth and ears of her parents.

Another explosion sounded. I smelled fire. But it was distant. I tensed my fists on my swords.

Just a bit longer.

"The soul is healed," she said, in a trance. Ignoring the explosions. "But the body is broken. But like any vessel, a body can be repaired."

She picked up the bottle of werewolf blood. Andy's blood. It was half empty. I guessed half of it was in the ritual circle.

"The regeneration of the wolf, tempered with the satisfaction of a vendetta fulfilled."

She poured the rest of the liquid over her parents' bodies. She then proffered what seemed to be a large white bird feather. She snapped it in half and placed half on each body.

"The feather of Seraphim, to balance the darkness and the light."

I no longer heard the undead. Just footfalls and shouting.

"Finally, the hearts of the healthy, given freely."

I didn't know how she accomplished that.

She placed the preserved human hearts on the chests of her parents.

The incantation that followed simultaneously sounded like the most beautiful symphony and the sound of abomination. Of chaos and order. Of life and death. She interwove both necromancy and healing words together. But that was impossible. She couldn't be. They were polar opposites. It was as if she was simultaneously allowing it to be day and night, in the same place at the same time. But she was doing it. And as it built in pitch and intensity, the immensity of what she was doing hit me. She was doing it. She was really doing it!

And I saw the hand of her father twitch, and clench. I dropped my swords but didn't hear them clatter. I fell to my knees, but Candace didn't stop.

The words were perfect. In perfect balance. Of light and dark. Of hate and love. Candace was right! The truth was to be found in both worlds. Which meant I was wrong…

She enunciated off the final words with a crescendo, and a wave of gold and green shot out, knocking me to the ground. The room fell silent. I lifted myself to my knees and watched the bodies. Watched them.

But nothing happened. No movement. No twitch.

"No…" Candace muttered, disbelieving. She repeated the final line. No magic lights. No crescendo. She repeated it again. And again. She screamed it. Then she just screamed. And she cried. She fell to the ground and beat the floor.

I was right, I realised.

It was impossible.

They were gone.

All of them.

Forever.

I crawled to her. Her hands were bloody and bruised. I touched her and she slapped at me, shouting. But I caught a glimpse of her eyes. There was no longer a veil of madness. There was only pain. I let her slap my hands away, and then I forced her into my arms. She struggled and pushed against me. But she weakened and wept into my chest.

"I miss them, Kat. I just want them back."

And I wish I had been wrong. That they could come back. That I could see Colin. That I could see my parents again. Just once.

"Me too," I answered. And I cried. For the first time in a long time. And I wept with my sister. For all our pain. And for all we had lost. Until the fire pushed against the door to the chamber and we dragged ourselves to our feet, vampires on our tail.

Candace was silent even as tears trailed down her face. She let out a slight yelp as she tripped over a fallen beam. She winced as she tried to stand up. I lifted her up and carried her. The stronghold was collapsing around us. My coat absorbed the flames, but it was too much. A vampire almost made it to us, but some of the ceiling caved in and blocked its path. We made it lower and lower, until the air was colder.

"We're almost there," I said, rasping.

Candace didn't reply.

I passed through the final door. And faced a pale woman with a cascade of black hair and wearing a leather bodysuit. Charlene Terhoff.

"Drummond," she hissed. I saw the glint of her fangs, despite the darkness of the room. Her eyes glowed red.

"Fuck off," I cried.

She advanced, her claws extending, just as the wall on both our sides exploded inward.

"Conrad?"

A man who looked like Conrad entered, wearing a brown leather coat and carrying a hand crossbow. Behind him was Cindy.

"Stay out of this!" Charlene roared.

I tried to put down Candace and draw my swords but realised that I had left them in the chamber. They were gone.

"I will handle this, Kat," Conrad said. He sounded, for the first time, truly menacing.

Charlene, her claws fully extended, charged at me. Before I could back out of the way, Conrad was in front of me, glowing a splendid white. Charlene's eyes widened and she froze, like a deer caught in headlights.

Wings of white and gold appeared from Conrad's back, stretching across the room, as he rose into the air.

He didn't look greasy. Or sleazy. Or like the salesman stereotype I knew him as. He was beautiful.

Charlene screamed as she tried to run, as each part of her body turned to dust. Piece by piece. She pulled herself along the floor as her legs disintegrated. Her torso caved, and then her arms. Until she was just a head. And then, just a pile of ash. A gust of wind blew what was left of her away.

The room went dark, and Conrad fell to his knees, looking human again. But much, much older. Cindy rushed to his side. He held up a hand to stop her.

"That was the last of it. I've expended my part of the deal."

He yawned. "I'm tired now."

"Conrad…" I whispered.

He smiled, weakly.

"Not the unveiling of my true form that I imagined."

"You…you're an angel?"

"Was. Not anymore."

"Thank you," I said. It was all I felt I could say. "For everything."

He nodded, and then stood, with Cindy's help. Her eyes drifted to Candace, who had her eyes closed, still in my arms.

"Who is she?"

Who was she? My friend. My sister. The Necrolord. A healer.

"A victim of necromancy," I said. "She's hurt. On the inside. But I think she can get better."

Cindy glared at Candace, but her features softened.

"I know a place she can stay. That will give her the help she needs."

"Thank you, Cindy."

"We're drawing a crowd, girls," Conrad said. "It's time we go."

I carried Candace out of the ruins of her stronghold, as Cindy helped Conrad.

Chapter 22. Blue Lights

Blue and red lights followed sirens. Conrad screeched to a halt on the ragged slum road as a line of police cars blocked our way.

I was in the car with Conrad, with him driving despite his apparent fatigue. Cindy was taking Candace somewhere else. We had anticipated the police and wanted to split up. Yet, I didn't anticipate this big of a reaction. Did they know that I killed a councillor's son? I couldn't feel much fear despite the danger. I was tired. Too tired. I just wanted to sleep.

The sirens didn't stop as police got out of their vehicles and levelled their guns at us. A familiar voice came over a megaphone.

"Kat Drummond. Get out of the vehicle or we will fire upon you."

James – fucking – Montague. And I thought we were friends.

I unbuckled my seatbelt. Conrad put his hand in front of me to stop me. I looked at him.

"This is my fault. No need for you to sacrifice more for me."

He kept his arm there.

James repeated. "Get out of the vehicle. This is your final warning."

I moved Conrad's arm out of the way and got out. My legs almost buckled, and I squinted into the harsh dawn sun rising above the rooftops.

"Drop your weapons," he ordered.

Only one weapons left. I unholstered Voidshot and placed it on the ground. Even from this distance, I saw the cops twitching. Would suit them to kill me by accident.

"Take off your fire coat."

I did so and felt a desperation come from my coat. It didn't want me to go. Neither did Treth, but he was also tired. Resigned. Like me.

My coat hissed as it hit the tarmac.

"Put your hands on your head and approach. Slowly."

I put them up and put one foot forward. Then the other. And the other. Lumbering. Not thinking.

Closer. Closer.

James dropped the megaphone and drew his service pistol. He pointed it at me as I came within around ten metres of the police line.

"Who could have fucking guessed that you were the one to kill Drake?" He spat. "You make me sick."

I didn't argue. What difference would it make? Ticks were stupid. Corrupt. They wouldn't listen. And I was too drained to even try.

"I have half the mind to kill you here myself."

I heard cars in the distance. Traffic. Life. Even in the slums. Always living. Breathing like an animal.

"Treason. Murder. Conspiracy. Theft," he glared at me as if his stare could kill. "Treachery."

I heard a click as he cocked back the hammer. What an outdated gun.

"The Spirit of the Law doesn't stretch this far. But mine does."

"Kat?" Treth asked. Yet, he also knew what was coming. And we were both tired. This was easier.

The black van totalled three cop cars as it rammed into them. In a single motion, Brett opened the car door, holding one of Guy's machine-pistols. He levelled it at James' head.

My eyes widened. He was injured. Arm bandaged. Burns. But he was alive. And so was I.

And I didn't want to die.

I heard a multitude of clicks as the police not hit in the crash aimed their guns at us.

"Brett…" I said. "You don't need to do this."

"I like this," James said. "All the fucking traitors in one place. And this far out, no court will even know what happened."

"But you'll be dead," Brett answered, his voice as cold as cast iron.

"And I will have served Hope City," he answered.

Nobody fired. They kept their guns levelled. No sound.

James opened his mouth and I could practically feel the surge of bullets as he shouted the order to fire.

But he didn't. He exploded in gore and organs. Brett and I jumped back as James' abandoned legs collapsed to the ground, his torso obliterated.

The cops didn't fire. They got right back into their police cars and sped off. None of them was prepared to fight mages.

I caught a glimpse of another's vision, staring down at me. I looked up with my own eye and saw a hooded figure duck down and disappear.

Chapter 23. Loss

There was no warrant for our arrest. They didn't know about Andy. The deaths of the hunters who helped me were chalked up to another job gone wrong. In a city full of man-eating monsters, the lack of bodies was accepted immediately.

James had been acting in a rogue capacity. And none of the cops that had joined him ever came forward. I suspected that they were just pawns of his, and when the king fell, they lost their protection and purpose. They went back into the ranks of Hope City's overpaid finest.

Candace had disappeared. Cindy claimed it happened while she stopped at a traffic light in the slums. One second, she was there, asleep. The next…gone. Cindy tried searching for her but couldn't find her anywhere. I didn't know where she went either. She didn't speak to me. I sometimes felt her presence, however. Watching me, as I sometimes watched her. She was in a hot, humid place. Filled with spices. She was still sad. And she missed me. But she knew that she had to learn to be alone. She felt a deep guilt for what she had done. And for the first time in a long time, she was truly awake.

The Sintari elves of northern New Zealand overran the last ANZAC troops at Christchurch. My aunt was MIA. Presumed dead. Just another person to mourn. Another body on the unlit pyre. I would cry for her…sometime. But I had cried enough.

Trudie was in hospital. I hadn't gone to visit her. I wasn't ready to face her yet. Pranish went instead. His phone was always off when he was with her, and his phone was almost always off these days.

I had, understandably, failed university. I decided not to go back. It was not my life. It didn't suit me, and I didn't suit it. But what was my life?

Treth had not scolded me. We hadn't spoken about the last while so far. I felt he hadn't forgiven me, yet. But also, that he didn't hate me. I still had him. But our relationship would be strained. At least for a while.

I sat on a cliff's edge, overlooking Hope City, as the sun-set behind me and the lights of the city came alive. I had been here once before. When I had killed Cornelius. Not my first kill. But perhaps the first one I regretted. It seemed as appropriate spot as any.

I heard crunching behind me but didn't turn until I felt cold glass on my cheek. I looked up to see Brett, holding two bottles of beer. He offered me one. I accepted it and drank, deeply.

He sat down, next to me and took a swig, and then sat with me for a short silence.

"Happy New Year, Kat," he finally said.

I didn't respond. I only watched the city. The cars. The houses. The businesses. My city. I said I would save it. But could it be saved? When its enemy was itself. When the monsters were endless. When the monsters were human.

"I thought I could save her," I said, finally and in almost a whisper.

"I think you did."

I shook my head. "No. I only helped her prove she was wrong. But she's still out there. And she's hurting."

"Is she hurting? Or are you?"

I looked at him, expecting to see a juvenile grin, but his eyes were serious. Half staring at me and half staring at something years in the past. Brett had felt pain. Had lost so much. Like me.

"Are we meant to lose?" I asked. "In the end? To watch everyone we love die? To see our friends hate us? To be killers who can never really save anything? To watch the world around us crumble even as we bleed every fucking drop to change something that can't be changed."

I clenched my fist and looked up at the sky, forcing my tears to remain unshed.

"Are we meant to lose everything?"

"No," he replied. "Not everything."

I looked at his face. His sadness. His resilience. I hadn't lost everything. And neither had he.

I looked back at the city, just as the magic show began, lights and illusions filled the sky, and my head found its way onto Brett's shoulder, where it stayed for the rest of the night.

Afterword

The world is not black and white. But neither is it merely grey. There are undeniable goods, undeniable bads, and there are a lot of things in between. Kat saw good in Candance, despite the evil that she had committed. And Kruger is a monster that keeps monsters in line.

There is black, and white, but also a lot of grey.

Darkness Beckons seems like a finale to many readers. It isn't. There's plenty of loose-ends and further stories to tell, but it is a conclusion to the first major arc in the series – what I dubbed the Necrolord Arc. But while some stories have reached their conclusions, Hope City is still brimming with evil, the Mentor is still out there, and there are still monsters to slay.

Until next time.

Sincerely,

Nicholas Woode-Smith.

Acknowledgements

This book would not have been possible to produce without the support of my family, notably my mother/proofreader. I must also give a lot of credit to Chelsea Murphy, who acts as my most active and enthusiastic beta reader.

Thank you to my friends who put up with my requests for cover critiques and to Deranged Doctor Design for making the covers.

Thank you to my D&D group, for inspiring a lot of what happens in these books.

Finally, thank you to you, the reader, for making this all possible.

Nicholas Woode-Smith is a full-time fantasy and science fiction author from Cape Town, South Africa. He has a degree in philosophy and economic history from the University of Cape Town. In his off-time, he plays PC strategy games, Magic: The Gathering, and Dungeons & Dragons.

Follow him on Facebook:

https://www.facebook.com/nickwoodesmith/

Made in the USA
Middletown, DE
27 March 2021